PETER S

THE JOKE THAT KILLED

🐕 THE BOOMER CREW 2 🐕

The Boomer Crew: The Joke That Killed

Published 2024

Copyright © Peter Seddon, 2024

The moral right of Peter Seddon to be identified as author of this work has been asserted in accordance with the Copyright, Designs and Patents Act 1988.

All rights reserved.

CHAPTER ONE

Money had always been scarce in the John household, and Finley felt sure the problem went back several generations. He could tell from looking at old family photos: from his grandfather to his father to his uncles and cousins, they all had the same look in their eyes, like they were staring through a cloud of unresolved maths. But Ella, just before she passed, had broken the spell and Finley could hardly believe it.

It was no surprise then that news of this miraculous £100,000 lottery win reached his children, but exactly how Lisa and Adam had found out, he wasn't sure. In this small town everybody heard the gossip, sooner or later. Marge at the post office probably told Judy, who no doubt mentioned it to her daughter, Penny, the lollipop lady. It figures that Penny may have congratulated Adam about his dad's good fortune as he passed her en route to his job at the butcher's. Adam's eyebrows would have risen and he'd have had to call his sister, who, after a quick convo, would have agreed that it was time they visited their old man. It had been a decade, after all.

'Sorry it's been a while,' Adam said, as he sat as far back on Finley's living room couch as he could.

'I'm sure you've been busy.' Finley did his best to cleanse the melancholy from his words, but feeling some latent emotion on his breath, he kept it short.

Lisa perched on the couch next to Adam. 'I'd have brought Mark over to see you but he's in school.'

'Mark?' Finley was almost too afraid to ask.

'You know Mark. He's seven now.'

Finley bit his lip. A father should know how to deal with this awkwardness, but when a solar eclipse comes around more often than a visiting family member, it's easy to get out of practice.

With a sigh he said, 'She was the glue that kept us together, wasn't she?'

'Who?' asked Adam.

'Your mother.' He looked at a picture of Ella he kept on a shelf. It was the order of service from her funeral and every day, for the last twelve years since her passing, he had looked to it for solace. She looked so happy in that photo. There she was, smiling back at him, her image fading into a white background. Lisa tilted her head to the picture. Adam elbowed her discreetly.

'So you've had some good luck, I hear?' she said, turning back to her dad.

'How's work?' Finley said at the same time, their overlapping words clashing like a rugby scrum.

Lisa nodded. 'Fine, yeah. I'm a manager now at the call centre. And Adam runs the butcher shop, don't you, Adam?'

'Aye.'

They fell into silence, as if plunged into different dimensions. Lisa looked at her feet.

Finley was desperate to come up with something to say, but he couldn't help noticing the seconds tick away on the mantel clock. The hand moved so agonisingly slowly he wondered if it was broken.

Building a bridge, his father once said, that's how you turn strangers into friends; you have to build a connection. But Finley was struggling to find the raw materials.

A car honked outside, startling them all. Finley turned to the window. On the road outside, Blakey waved from the driver's seat of his car.

'Sorry. I've got to go,' Finley said. 'I have an appointment I can't miss. Well, it's more of a meeting, really. Something I can't get out of.' He hated to cut the visit short.

Adam and Lisa rose slowly from the couch, too busy exchanging glances to respond.

'Okay,' Lisa said eventually, swinging her arms in her warm-looking overcoat. 'We better get off too. It was nice to see you.'

'You too. Both of you.' Finley said, unsure of what goodbye etiquette to employ.

Blakey's car horn blasted again.

'We'll be seeing you, Dad.' Adam turned to exit and Lisa followed him out of the door.

'You know you can come back and visit again if you want to?' Finley said.

Lisa popped her head back through the door frame.

'Yeah,' she said. 'I'd like that.'

CHAPTER TWO

A swirl of litter greeted them in the snooker hall's car park. Loose newspaper pages danced in the dust and brushed against the building's graffiti-splashed walls. There was only one other car parked: a Rolls-Royce Silver Shadow with glistening bodywork, sleek chrome accents and dark tinted windows. It lay there like a lion in a desert, and with its 'MRB1GG' reg plate and gleaming bonnet-mounted statue it was an otherworldly monument amid the council estate dereliction. A clear statement of power and prestige.

With a door slam, Finley exited Blakey's mustard-coloured Ford Mark II Escort.

'You sure about this?' Blakey said as he followed suit.

Finley shook his head. 'We've not much choice. Like you said, when Mr Bigg summons you, you better show up.'

It was clear to Blakey that Finley would rather be elsewhere, and not just for the obvious reason. Having always been simpatico, he could tell there was something else on Finley's mind. But now was not the time to ask. He figured it was something to do with the visitors he'd seen in Finley's flat, but Finley wasn't for talking on the ride over. His kids, Blakey assumed. Complicated.

Gottfried – or Geoff as he's better known to his pals – braced himself with a tug of his flat cap and ambled out of the car. Together, the three of them trudged across the car park while a group of kids shouted at each other at a bus stop across the street. The wind bristled and the occasional car whooshed by and drowned out the noise of their shoes on the broken concrete.

Geoff blew out his cheeks. 'Who the heck would want to play snooker in a place like this? It's hardly welcoming, is it?'

Blakey nodded as he scanned the entrance. Two large bay windows surveyed them, their glare narrowed by plywood boards. To the right of the entrance was a small window with the words 'Mr Bigg's Snooker Club' faded on the pane. A small neon sign on the door flickered and struggled against the afternoon daylight. 'Snooker'.

'This place has been here since the 60s,' Blakey said in an attempt to break the tension. 'But Charlie says it's now just a front for the mob, and the off-putting decor is intended to keep customers away.'

With a final glance over their shoulder, they walked inside to a reception area, which was empty aside from a vending machine offering hot drinks. The thing smelled rancid and the buttons were covered in dirt. The main hall was no better; the stench of stale urine and old cigarette smoke hit the back of Blakey's throat as he walked in. There was no clink of snooker balls – just row after row of empty tables lit from above by lamps that perfectly framed their green cloth, giving them a luminous glow against the surrounding shadows.

Blakey felt his blood run cold as he wondered how Charlie, his grandson and semi-professional footballer, knew so much about this place. Probably from urban legends, he told himself. Probably. Despite his anxiety, Blakey refused to be scared; at the age of 74, he'd been around the block too many times to be spooked by a dilapidated old building.

'Blakey,' Geoff whispered, 'tell me again how you know Harry the Hammer.'

'I don't *know* him. I've just heard about him.'

'Why do they call him Harry the Hammer?'

'Let's just say it's not because he likes DIY.'

Blakey ran his hand down the soft wool cloth of a snooker table, his fingertips grazing the nicks and cuts in the surface. Geoff hung back while Finley turned his attention to the walls and studied the black-and-white posters covering them. Most of them were images of boxers slugging it out in the ring; some were flyers advertising fights from yesteryear.

Finley's style had changed since his lotto win a few months ago. Instead of wrapping up in the same worn-out winter coat all year round, he now sported plush Saville Row padded jackets – he had one in green and a few in navy. His breath smelled of mint and his clothes were scented with the spicy, woody aroma of an expensive cologne. He'd even had his eyes checked and come out with a pair of Hugo Boss glasses, which fit with his new high-end barbershop hairstyle and freshly groomed grey stubble. It was all a little posh for Blakey's taste, but he couldn't deny Finley made being in his seventies look cool, especially with his mischievous grin, which gave him the air of someone who could finally afford to take things easy.

Finley strolled the length of the wall, stopping abruptly at one poster. He squinted intently at it, his hands hanging motionless at his side.

'Well bugger me,' he said. 'I *do* know Harry the Hammer, after all. Look at this.' He pointed to the poster. 'This fight – you'll remember this one – it was an all-time classic: "Mad Dog" John Jones versus Harry "the Hammer" Bigg for the British heavyweight title, 1964.'

A gruff voice came from the shadows.

'Gentlemen.'

Blakey stood by the glow of a snooker table. Geoff's eyes darted towards the sound of heavy footsteps. Sharp angles of light cast across a well-suited figure approaching them. The confident clicks of leather against wooden floor echoed as Blakey unconsciously pressed himself against the table's edge.

Finley eyes still were still on the poster, his hands still at his side.

The man appeared in the dim glow between two tables and from his appearance, Blakey got the message that this was a person not to be messed with. He had a timeless intimidating style, and he towered over them. Maybe it was his pronounced jaw or his slicked-back silver hair or perhaps his neatly pressed three-piece suit (complete with pocket watch), but he clearly meant business. And the two large men in the shadows behind him didn't hurt his aura either.

'Allow me to introduce myself,' the man said in a coarse northern voice.

Finley shook his head. 'You don't need to tell me who you are, mate.' He pointed to the poster. 'I remember that fight. What a belter that was. The way you took that beating then got up in the sixth and knocked his block off. Only Harry the Hammer could do that.'

Harry smiled. 'Very kind of you. You know it's funny,' he pointed at the poster, his large, bulbous hand adorned with the biggest signet ring Blakey had ever seen. 'When I was a lad, my dad would always say to me, "Son, with a temper like yours, you need to be a boxer, cos it's either that or the nick for you".' A smile grew on his face. 'But truth be told, I was never much of a fighter until I got mad. But like I used to tell the press, when someone upsets me I can't be held responsible for my actions.'

'And this is a picture of you beating Crusher Barstow in Las Vegas, isn't it?' Finley said.

'Course.'

'And is it true you dated Twiggy?' Finley pointed at a paparazzi pic of Harry and the model arm in arm.

'I had to tell her to do one. She wouldn't leave me alone. Anyway, as much as I'd like to reminisce, we have an urgent piece of business to discuss, so gentlemen, step into my office.'

He directed their attention to a softly lit office in the back.

CHAPTER THREE

Harry's office made Blakey uncomfortable and the lack of light made him squint, but from the warm glow of the room's one desk lamp, he could see it was immaculate. There was a faint scent of leather from the many boxing gloves on display behind Harry's desk. There was also a large painting of Harry dressed like a nobleman from Elizabethan England, framed in shining gold and hung on the wall behind his chair. The rest of the room was clad floor to ceiling in deep mahogany, like a library in a British detective story. Blakey preferred spaces like his garage: the concrete floor, the tools and the well-worn spot for his mug next to the radio on his workbench were just enough to be comfortable. The only tool that Blakey could see in Harry's office was a hammer. A pristine, polished-silver claw hammer set out on Harry's desk next to a whisky glass that glittered in the light. It was as if the two were intended to be used together.

Geoff stood at the door, looking like he was about to run, while Finley prowled the room, taking it all in. Blakey slumped gracelessly into the chair in front of Harry's desk, mostly due to the arthritis in his knees flaring up again, but also because he wanted to get this over with. Harry sat on his throne of a chair and clasped his hands, his face an unreadable mask.

'Now, boys. You had a little run-in at the bank the other month, didn't you?'

Blakey's throat felt suddenly dry, as if he'd been sucking on a handful of sand. He let out a ragged breath. 'We had a little tête-à-tête with a young fella, you might say. If that's what you mean? These things happen, you know. The younger generation …'

'It was a bit more than a tête-à-tête,' Harry said, opening a drawer and flopping a copy of the *Glebe Observer* on the desk. 'Heroes: that's what the local media are calling you.' He leaned back.

'Bloody right we are,' Finley said as he admired a golden boxing glove mounted on a plinth at the back of the room. 'That young lad was trying to rob the place with a machete! He even held Geoff hostage, but we stopped him.'

Geoff shrugged nonchalantly but his eyes were shifting rapidly. 'It was nothing. Just right time, right place.'

'No. Wrong time. Wrong place,' Harry growled. Finley spun around on hearing Harry's tone.

Harry leaned forward. 'That young lad was on a little job for me, see. And thanks to your *heroic* efforts, not only is the young boy in the nick, but now out I'm of pocket.'

'That's nothing to do with us,' Blakey said.

Geoff gulped. 'Blakey's right. That's not our fault.'

'This is a very serious matter,' Harry declared.

Finley took a seat next to Blakey. 'Mr Hammer, er, Mr Bigg. How is this our problem? I mean, if your boy was any good, he'd have done the job right and you'd have your money, no problem.'

Geoff took a step into the room, tense and ready to speak. 'By the way, that lad you set up is called Butler. And he happens to be my girlfriend's grandson, so, Mr Bigg, I really think you ought to leave him alone. Butler's not well and we're doing our best to help him.'

'I can see what you're saying,' Harry said, reclining in his chair. 'He's always been a soft lad, has that young Butler. Regardless, if it wasn't for you three, all that stood in his way was that creep of a bank manager, Derek Onions, and he's hardly likely to put up a fight, is he? Be quivering under his desk, most likely. We all agree, you did stop the robbery, that much is clear, so according to my calculations, based on the size of the bank, you boys owe me twenty-five big ones.'

Geoff burst. 'Bugger me!'

Blakey nearly slipped off his chair.

Finley leaned forward. 'You need a new calculator Harry, cos we can't be liable for that!'

Blakey composed himself. 'Come on, Harry, you can't seriously expect us to pay you twenty-five grand. It's not our fault your job went wrong.'

Harry picked up the hammer off his desk and smiled. 'Good boy, your lad Charlie is, isn't he? Shame if something was to impede his football career. Bad injury or scandal.'

Blakey bolted to his feet, his chest beating. 'Don't you dare bring my grandson into this. It's bad enough you're trying to shake us down, but you have no business involving Charlie.'

Harry set down his hammer and walked to a drinks cabinet in the corner. The sound of ice cubes dropping into glasses followed. Harry returned with tumblers filled with whisky and passed a drink to each man. Blakey couldn't take his eye off the massive ring on Harry's finger. It was solid gold and stamped with the letters 'HH', as if it were designed to brand those he had reason to strike.

'I am nothing if not reasonable,' Harry said, sitting back down. 'I can see that you boys are the same as me, really. We're cut from the same cloth. We're old fashioned and we like the old ways: honesty, hard work … and paying off your debts.'

'Do you know how much a pension is these days? It's not much,' Geoff said. 'How do you expect us to come up with twenty-five grand?'

'That part's easy.' Harry set down his drink and clasped his hands. 'I got a job for you.'

'A job?' Blakey said.

'A job,' Harry grinned. 'A favour to square off this difficult situation.'

Blakey took a large shot of whisky; the aroma of fire and honey engulfed his senses. 'No.' He choked back the burn. 'I'm retired. We all are, so we're not in the job market.'

'In that case, I'm sure young Charlie can take a small break from his meteoric rise to football stardom and help me out. He's a very talented lad. Very reasonable to deal with, too …'

Blakey wanted to grab Harry by the throat and throw him over the table, but he knew that it would only make things worse. Besides, Harry was massive up close. Blakey clamped his teeth and stopped himself inflaming the situation further.

Finley slammed his glass on the desk. 'You've got a nerve, Harry, and I'm sure you could eat me for dinner but I don't like the way you're threatening my mate and his grandson. Sure, you have us at a disadvantage – what with your influence and the cronies waiting outside – but if you weren't Harry the Hammer, I'd knock your bloody block off.' Finley's voice rose to a yell. *'Now what's the bloody job?* If we've no choice, I want to get it over with.'

'That's the spirit,' Harry boomed. 'You don't find mettle like that often these days. They don't make 'em like they used to, that's for sure. This job will be easy for fellas like you.'

'Does it really need all three of us?' Finley said. 'I'll take this one for the team.'

'Finley …' Blakey said.

'You and Geoff have been good to me. I owe both of you one, so I don't mind stepping up to help out.'

'Nice sentiment,' Harry said, 'But I'm afraid the job is going to need all three of you, so listen up. Here's the plan …'

CHAPTER FOUR

'Can you believe that nonsense?' Geoff yelped as they got back into Blakey's car. His face was blood red and the toe of his shoe thumped the car's footwell. 'Can't you buy him off with your money, Finley? I mean, of all the madness – what he's asking is ridiculous!'

Finley cleaned his glasses with a handkerchief and frowned. 'Where's the fun in that? Besides, what I've got left has to last me a lifetime. Match-day VIP treatment at Glebe Town don't come for free, you know.'

'Yes, it does! To you, at least,' Geoff said.

'It doesn't matter. It's a different kind of debt, this. He wants more than money out of us,' Finley sighed. 'Although it amounts to the same thing: servitude.'

Geoff pulled the flat cap off his head and wrung it. 'Blakey, you've not said a word. Come on, be the voice of reason here. We can't be working for the mob … what he's asking us to do is criminal. We can't do this. We'll go down for it. Straight to the nick. Oh, I ought to go back to Germany. It's only been forty years since I left but I'm sure it'll be much the same–'

'Calm down,' Finley said. 'Take it from me: debt you can't control will eat you alive if you let it.'

Blakey took several deep breaths. He didn't know what to say, so he started the car. The rumble of the engine startled a flock of pigeons on the tarmac in front of them.

As the birds flurried away, their wings flapped like an ironic applause.

'We're doing it,' Blakey said, pushing away thoughts of Charlie. He had to protect his grandson and he couldn't have Harry using his name like a threat. He cruised out of the car park, past the hoodies at the bus stop and drove away from the snooker hall in dreadful silence.

'For crying out bloody loud,' Finley said, breaking the atmosphere. He nudged Geoff and kicked the back of Blakey's seat. 'Tell us a bloody joke, you misery-guts! This isn't the end of the world.'

Geoff frowned out of the window and Blakey looked dead ahead.

Finley rolled his eyes. 'Okay, you asked for it … What does a man with a two-foot penis have for breakfast?' He looked for a reaction. 'Well, I'll tell you when you bloody cheer up, you old sods! We've only got a little job to do. A little, tiny job that's basically worth twenty-five grand. It's not that bad, if you think about it. It's not like we have to kill anyone … I mean, not really…'

CHAPTER FIVE

The Glebe Civic Centre was bustling as people poured into the theatre, their faces alive with anticipation as they entered the brightly lit auditorium, drinks clutched in hands, their colourful clothing creating a vibrant mosaic. Laughter and conversation spiced the air as music played in the background. By 7 p.m. almost all of the theatre's three hundred velvet seats were occupied as the house lights dimmed and the evening's entertainment began with a drum roll.

'I can't believe we're about to do this, I really can't.' Geoff rubbed his neck with such fervour it looked like he was trying to throttle himself. He stopped and looked at Blakey. 'Hold on … what are we supposed to do again?'

'Just follow my lead,' Finley said, 'and be quiet. It'll be a cracking show this. This fella's a right laugh.'

Blakey felt a mix of fear and excitement: despite the job they had to do, he also wanted to soak up the glamour of the theatre, especially since he hadn't seen anything this highbrow in a long time. They sat in the front-row seats Harry had reserved for them.

A voice came over the PA to introduce the star of the show. 'Ladies and gentlemen, please welcome your friend and mine, all the way from Tickle Valley, the one and only – Johnny Crackers!'

Red velvet curtains parted and the spotlight hit the stage, illuminating a sign: 'Johnny Crackers' Funny Hour'.

A bow-tied, red-suited man stepped towards a microphone.

'Wotcha, you bunch of wankers!' The crowd rolled with laughter. 'It's me, your favourite potty mouth, Johnny Crackers. Eee, it's been a long day, I tell thee. You know, after a long day, my favourite thing to do is sit down and take off my clothes – it makes the train ride home much more entertaining! Eeee, calm down, ladies.'

He towered over the crowd at only four feet and five inches tall, and the people threw their heads back and guffawed on cue as he rolled out a catalogue of catchphrases and below-the-belt punchlines.

But Blakey's nerves started to rise. He kept re-checking his watch. The time was approaching …

'Eee, you'll never believe it, what's the world coming to? You know I went to my local shop the other day to buy some rolling tobacco. "Shag?" the shopkeeper replied. What a kind offer, I thought, so I took off my trousers and he had me arrested!'

Finley laughed along with the crowd as they enjoyed the night. But the longer it went on, the more Blakey's mind started to drift.

'So then I went in the butcher's and asked for some bacon. "Lean back," he said. "Why?" I said. "My breath's not that bad."'

Blakey tuned out the comedian, catching only fragments of jokes, and couldn't help but watch the minutes tick away. The time was coming when he would have to make a choice … but what choice did he really have? Johnny Crackers' coarse red tartan suit, his overbearing tone, his post-punchline cackle mixed with the raucous laughter of the crowd. Blakey began to feel sick and his mind started to fray at the edges.

'So I nipped into the travel agent's to see at how much it costs to swim with dolphins. "Bloody 'ell," I said, "that's expensive". "It's cheaper than swimming with sharks," the agent said, "that really does cost an arm and a leg".'

One punchline after another, Johnny threw his head back and howled with the revellers as the crowd screamed with wild, tipsy laughter, until suddenly, Johnny clutched his chest, his eyes bulged, and his face contorted as if he'd just seen the devil himself. The blood drained from his face and he fell to the floor like an old chimney stack and a microphonic boom whined through the loudspeakers.

'He's collapsed!' shouted a woman in the crowd.

Finley bolted to his feet. 'Bloody hell! He's only gone and done the old Tommy Cooper!' He raced to the stage as the audience stood and gasped. Finley checked Johnny over then pleaded into the microphone, 'Is there a doctor in the house?'

Geoff glanced at Blakey and beckoned to him with urgency.

'Oh, bugger me,' Blakey whispered. He stood up and declared, 'Yes. I am a doctor. Allow me to assist.' He had been rehearsing the line in his head. Ascending the stage steps in front of three hundred worried faces, he hoped that no one among them would recognise him. Because if anyone did, they would know full well that he was no doctor.

The show had begun.

CHAPTER SIX

Gasps from the audience persisted as Blakey heaved himself on to the stage's polished wooden floor. His heart pounded – mostly because of the stress of the moment but also because of the exertion. Damn the arthritis. The gasps morphed into whispered exchanges as Blakey stepped into the dazzling white spotlight where Johnny Crackers' crumpled body lay.

Finley stood over Johnny and signalled for Blakey to perform his doctorly duties as Geoff eventually joined them on stage. Looking out beyond the stage lights, Geoff's eyes darted across the crowd. He looked dumbfounded, stumblefuzzed. A bead of sweat ran down his cheek and he stood transfixed, helplessly rooted to the spot.

Blakey knelt to attend to Johnny, in a way he expected a doctor would, but he was nervous. He had never checked a pulse before. He'd seen it done on TV and he knew it was somewhere in the neck or the wrists, but Johnny's outfit made it difficult to find. The stiff weave of the tartan seemed moulded to his body; the cuffs and collars were tight against his skin, preventing access to anywhere pulseworthy. In a panic, Blakey put a hand on Johnny's forehead and counted steadily.

'Anything?' Finley said.

'I dunno …' Blakey shrugged. A flutter of voices rippled through the audience.

'There's only one thing for it,' Finley said. He shot Blakey a look. 'You have to give him mouth-to-mouth.'

Blakey gulped. 'Oh dear,' he whispered. He looked at Johnny's face, took a deep breath and aimed for the lips.

Johnny's mouth twitched. 'Don't you bloody dare ...' he muttered. 'Just get me off this stage, you old bollock ... and act like I'm dead.'

'Righto.' Finley approached the mic and addressed the crowd.

'Er, sorry, lads and lasses, but the wee fella's dead. Deader than Diana, I'm afraid. Sorry. We'll be off now.'

This triggered a chorus of, 'What did he just say?' and 'Ya wat?' Ignoring them, Finley grabbed Johnny's tartan arms and Blakey grabbed his tartan legs. The arthritis in Blakey's knees really started to flare up as they carted Johnny off stage like an old bathtub, but Geoff was still frozen on stage, his eyes wide with horror, staring at the crowd as their collective disbelief grew in volume.

'Geoff!' Finley hissed. 'Stop looking at them and get off stage.'

But Geoff seemed unable. The most he could do was let out a high-pitched hum, which was picked up by the microphone and caused everyone to stare even harder. The audience got to their feet en masse and swathes of people swept towards him like a tide, gathering across the front row, inches from his feet.

Once beyond the wing curtains, Finley dropped Johnny like a wonky wheelbarrow and raced back to help Geoff, grabbing his arm and dragging him away to the relative safety of backstage before the gathering mob could claim him.

CHAPTER SEVEN

They made a quick getaway via the stage door as a perfect shroud of confusion settled on the audience and the venue staff alike.

Blakey's heart raced with nervous energy as he drove away from the crime scene, and soon his Ford was creeping onto the winding private road leading to Finley's flat. At this time of night, in the car's dim headlights, the road was an unnerving mix of shadows with the occasional lamppost casting a hazy glow over them before darkness swallowed them again.

Still shaken by his on-stage debut, Blakey's embarrassment bubbled to the surface as the terrible tension melted away. He had no idea how the actors on *Casualty* managed to act like doctors all day. He'd barely managed sixty seconds and he'd felt foolish the whole time.

'Turn off the headlights,' Finley said as they sneaked further across the court. 'We don't want anyone noticing us.' Blakey was in no mood to argue, so he did as he was told.

'Good lad.'

The darkness ahead loomed like a solid wall, so Blakey slowed even more.

'We're almost there, just a little further on,' Finley said. 'Be careful you don't knock over my bird feeder.'

'Did you see them all back there?' Geoff said hazily, as if still in a trance. 'Hundreds of them … hundreds of eyes all staring right through me. They could see something was afoot.'

'A foot and a body, I reckon.' Finley chortled. 'They just watched Johnny Crackers kick the bucket live on stage. They didn't know what hit them.'

A muffled protest came from the boot of the car.

'I think Johnny's had enough of being in the boot, by the sounds of it,' Blakey said as he eased to a halt in front of Finley's door.

'No,' said Geoff, 'I mean they knew something was up with *us*. What if somebody recognised us? It'll be a police matter, a public death like that. And the *Glebe Observer* will be all over it.'

'Harry's got that covered, remember?' Finley said. 'Like he told us, it's nothing a few pound notes stuffed into the right pockets can't sort.'

Another muffled shout and a series of dull thuds boomed from the boot.

'Alright, Johnny,' Finley said. 'Let me check the coast is clear and I'll sneak you inside.'

CHAPTER EIGHT

Rachael Ribbons woke to the sound of her phone vibrating off her couch and hitting the floor. Groggy, leery, she didn't want to speak to anyone, especially anyone from the office. It was Friday night, for crying out loud. Couldn't they leave her alone for one evening? She had only recently been promoted junior editor, a reward given after her piece about the Hip Replacement Bandits went national. Or maybe the promotion was a punishment? She couldn't tell.

One thing she was certain of was that keeping on top of the news was exhausting. Tonight, like most nights, she had fallen asleep on the sofa before nine p.m., too tired to finish her glass of Yellow Tail chardonnay. In her old life as an on-the-beat reporter, her work was done when the story was sent to the editor's inbox, which was usually three p.m. She missed that. Now, her inbox was the one all the reporters were submitting to before they nip off to the pub.

She picked her head up from the cushion. Sweeping her hair from her face, she searched the carpet for her phone. BBC iPlayer was still playing episodes of *Luther* on her TV, but she wasn't concerned about missing an episode: she'd already binged it several times.

She found her phone just as it stopped buzzing. The call was from Gina, her boss. It was almost ten p.m. Reassuring herself that she was definitely off the clock, she swiped the notification away, only to notice six other missed calls, two voice messages and three texts, all from Gina.

I bet Naga Munchetty doesn't have to deal with this, she thought as the phone rang again. Gina's never one to make a social call. Doesn't she realise the time?

'Hi, Gina.' Rachael yawned through her hand. 'Yeah, I think I've have heard of Johnny Crackers. A comedian, right? He's a little before my time. Can this wait?'

'Not really,' Gina replied.

'Okay, but he's not really *Observer* material.'

'He might be now. At least for the obituary section...'

'Oh ... he's dead?'

'As a door nail. Collapsed on stage a couple hours ago, apparently.'

'Wait, if this is an obituary piece, why are you calling me? This sounds like a job for Ralph.'

'Because there's something fishy about it, although I can't figure out what. Some early witness accounts from the Civic Centre – and by that, I mean my husband – said when a doctor was asked for, a few elderly men came out of the crowd and approached the stage, and one of them had a very familiar flat cap ...'

'Flat cap? You mean ... Geoff?'

'John recognised him, at least his hat, from the photo attached to your piece about the Hip Replacement Bandits. He couldn't really place the other two fellas, but I'm going to guess they were Geoff's cohorts, Blakey and Finley – from what you've told me, those three are inseparable.'

'Yeah.'

'So anyway, they all got on stage and in no time they announced that Johnny was dead. Then they carted him off stage, which doesn't sound very professional for a doctor, does it? But then again, none of those guys are actually doctors, are they?'

Rachael racked her brain. No. None of them were or had ever been a medical professional. And she should know: she'd written their bios for her article.

Gina continued. 'What's more, there'll be no investigation or police inquiry, from what I've been told. You'd at least expect a police coroner to be involved to ascertain the cause of death – that's a minimum legal requirement – but no. Officer Anders says there's no need for such an inquiry. And that's exactly the kind of thing gets me wondering.'

'Wondering what?'

'Perhaps it's time you paid your old pals a visit. They know something. And even if they don't, there's a story here, I can feel it.'

It sounded like a pointless line of enquiry, a total 'nothing burger', and besides, she was a junior editor now, not a reporter working the beat.

'I know what you're thinking,' Gina said. 'You're an editor now, not a reporter on the beat, and yes that's right. But I want your experience on this, and your instinct, so I'll get someone to cover your position while – oh dear, you seen the time? Must go. Keep me updated.'

Rachael reached for her glass of room-temperature vino and felt a smile grow on her lips. Editing really wasn't for her anyway. She'd much rather be back in the field.

CHAPTER NINE

'I think we got away with that,' Finley said, looking out of the flat's window into the darkness of the court beyond. 'Daisy next door would have seen us come in: she doesn't miss a thing. But she's alright, and I'm sure Geoff will clue her in.'

'Who's she? Some silly old bugger like you?' Johnny walked around the flat, opening drawers, looking at Finley's records and sneering at Ella's picture.

'You're a lot funnier on stage, aren't you?' Finley said as he turned on his hi-fi and slipped on a Mark Knopfler record. 'Make yourself comfortable. You'll be spending the night here.' He dropped the stylus and the sound of slow clean guitar meandered through the flat as Johnny walked off into the kitchen. Finley followed just as Johnny opened the fridge and helped himself to a can of Carlsberg.

'What a night,' Johnny said as he cracked the can open and chugged it in one. 'What's your story?' he said as he reached for another beer.

'I don't have one,' Finley said, folding his arms and leaning against the door frame.

'Give over. Everybody has a story. Explain yourself,' Johnny said mid-burp.

'I don't have to explain myself,' Finley said, grabbing a can of his own.

'Old fellas are so boring,' Johnny said.

'I don't explain myself and I don't expect others to either,' Finley said. 'None of us have time for explaining.' Finley took a swig. 'That was some performance on stage tonight. The heart attack bit looked like part of the act, it was so well done.'

'All men dream of their own doom,' Johnny said, finishing his beer and grabbing yet another. 'All we crave is an audience.'

'That's a bleak outlook, pal.'

'Least I went out on a high.'

Finley scoffed.

'Well, maybe not a high but at least I still had a crowd – not the biggest, but still. And now I've got Harry and his bloody hammer to deal with. Consider tonight my end-of-the-world party.'

'Not in my gaff,' Finley said.

Johnny loosened his tie. 'I'm going to enjoy what time I've got left.'

Johnny gulped his beer.

'Calm down,' Finley said. 'It ain't all that bad. Besides, you agreed to this. Harry mentioned you have some issues with the Inland Revenue that he's going to take care of, if you play along. He also said he'd wipe the slate in terms of what you owe him.'

Finley retreated to the living room and turned up his favourite song on this LP.

'You don't know anything,' Johnny said, following Finley into the living room. 'If you did, you'd leave me to it.'

'Leave you to do what? Drink all my beer?'

'Leave me to dying. I've had it. I just can't go through with this. I know what the deal was, but I can't do it. I mean it. I can't handle this debt anymore! So it might as well end for me now!'

Finley shook his head. 'Shut up and tell a bloody joke.'

Johnny took another slug of beer. 'What does a man with a two-foot penis have for breakfast?'

Before Finley could claim ownership of that particular joke, Johnny bolted back to the kitchen. The sound of doors knocking and drawers slamming forced Finley to make haste into the kitchen, where he found Johnny with a bottle of pills in hand, ones taken from Finley's medicine drawer. Johnny ripped the cap off the container and munched down a handful of white tablets.

'Goodbye, you old git. Goodbye, cruel world. This is it for me.'

Finley folded his arms again, rolling his eyes. 'Vitamin C won't kill you, but it might give you the trots.'

Johnny spat the half-chewed pills onto the countertop and seized a bottle of bleach from the cabinet under the sink.

'This'll do the job!'

Finley lunged at the bottle. 'You're going too far now! Calm down, you bugger, and put the bottle down.'

Johnny paused, his hand on the lid, staring at Finley. 'I wish I had a dad like you.'

'My dad had hands like a leather shovel and he'd have soon seen to you.'

'That's not what I meant. I did have a dad, nobhead. I mean, I wish my dad was *like* you. Cool and calm, like.'

'Mind your language, young man.'

Johnny twisted the lid and wrestled with the security cap. Finley grabbed hold and tried to pull it away, but Johnny held it to his chest and clung on for dear life until his face grew red and he threw it to the floor.

'Bollocks to it,' he said as the bottle rolled across the lino. 'Where's the whisky, pops?'

'Some house guest you are,' Finley said. 'Now enough.' He led him to the drinks cabinet in the living room and pulled out a bottle of Bunnahabhain single malt.

He smiled at Johnny, whose tight tartan blazer was stained chalky white from chewed-up vitamin C.

'This stuff's better than bleach,' Finley said, handing over a glass of booze. 'Not as good for you as vitamin C, according to some, but it'll still cure what ails you.'

Johnny's hangdog look had begun to soften Finley's heart.

Johnny shot back the liquor. 'My brother was always the smart one,' he said, sitting on the arm of Finley's chair and wiping down his blazer. 'I always thought he was just a geek. Never had a girlfriend at school, you know. I was always the funny one, the popular one. But now here I am, bound for jail no matter what I do. This debt situation is dreadful. I have two options: go to jail for five years for tax evasion or let Harry pay off my debts and take my brother's place in prison for the remaining ten months of his sentence. Either way, I am headed behind bars. How come he's the one that everyone cares about? Who'd have thought anyone would give a crap about my brother? He may be my twin, but he's a boring old nobody. He's just a high-street chemist, a nerd, for crying out loud.'

'He's not just any chemist though, is he?' Finley reclined in his chair. 'And he appears to be very important to Harry. But smart as he is, it didn't keep him out of trouble now, did it? So don't fret, you're still funnier and more popular than him, I'll bet.'

Johnny stared into his glass. 'It doesn't matter now, does it? People think I'm dead. What am I supposed to do when this is all over? How does a dead comedian make a comeback?'

Finley smiled. 'With a tell-all, must-read interview in a tabloid, of course. Think of the headline: Comic Back From the Dead. Think of what that will do for ticket sales.'

A smile appeared on Johnny's face.

'That's something that's not been done before. A comeback from the dead ... not even Bob Monkhouse could have pulled that one off.' Johnny rubbed his chin as Finley topped up his glass. 'I could sell out Blackpool ballroom with that idea. I'd be back with a bang! I might even get the Daz Challenge TV ads back off whatshisface. Big earner, that is. And maybe I'd get a spot on *I'm a Celeb*. Then daytime TV here I come. I'll be on *Loose Women* in no time!'

'Aye, lad.' Finley pressed the button to raise the footrest of his electric armchair. 'There's just the matter of a little job we need to do first, then we're home free …'

CHAPTER TEN

The night sky was starless and unrelenting. The moon was obscured behind a haze and cast the street in an eerie, diffuse light. His watch read ten p.m. Blakey grimaced at the thought of calling on Charlie at such an unsociable hour but after Harry had used his name so liberally, he needed to talk.

He hesitated at the garden's threshold, wondering exactly how he'd raise his concerns. Still unsure, he stepped between the pair of stone lions that sat on the edge of the driveway. He shook his head. Plinths with lions on are all very well, he thought, but the houses they sit outside of don't come cheap. And as for the brand-new Range Rover on the driveway, Charlie must have more money than sense.

The gravel crunched under his feet as he approached the property's lavish faux-Georgian exterior and knocked on the door. The sound of his knuckles on the hard wood echoed like a gunshot. His worry threatened to spill over with every second he had to wait. After what felt like an eternity, the door creaked open revealing Robin, Charlie's girlfriend, standing in her pyjamas, a bewildered look on her face.

'Ay up, love. How you feeling?' Blakey said.

She blew strands of auburn hair from her eyes. 'Nobody ever told me morning sickness can kick in at night,' she winced.

'Oh dear. How many weeks is it now?'

'Only twelve, so there's a long way to go yet.' She wiped her brow. 'This is a funny time for you to call.'

'Sorry. I didn't realise it was so late.' He felt bad about lying. 'Is Charlie about?'

'Yeah. You better come in out of the dark.' She hitched up the knot of her dressing gown and waved him in. 'He's upstairs, building a flatpack we got for the baby's room. He's been on it for three hours. I've told him we've got plenty of time yet but he wants everything to be sorted asap.'

Blakey checked his watch. 'It's a bit late for him to be building flatpacks.'

'He says he won't be beaten, but I think he could use a little help from his grandad right about now.'

'Okie dokie,' he said, rubbing his hands together. 'Show me at it.'

Blakey loved the fact that Charlie was terrible at DIY. It was something he could trust Charlie to make a mess of, which would usually lead to a phone call and a plea for help.

The grandeur of Charlie and Robin's new place still astonished Blakey. Especially when ambiently lit, like it was now. The polished marble floor and sweeping oak staircase that rose from the centre of the reception looked like something from a classic movie. *Gone With The Wind*, maybe, if it was set in the north of England. This room alone was vast – you could park a camper van between the door and the staircase, which meant Blakey usually felt like he ought to jog towards the stairs, just to speed things up. But Robin was leading the way and he felt it would be in poor taste to race a pregnant woman even early in her first term, especially because he would definitely win. With her shuffling slowly across the floor in a pair of slippers, it would be an easy victory.

She eventually reached the banister and rested her arm on it. Blakey paused at the foot of the stairs and squinted into the darkness. The only light on the landing was a faint glint of moonlight filtering through a small window.

'Eeee, it's like the black hole of Calcutta in here,' he said.

Robin mopped her brow. 'Asher. Turn on the staircase lights.'

'I'll get them, love. Hold on, who's Asher?' Blakey looked about. Perhaps they had hired a butler with Charlie's goal bonus money? A ghostly monotone voice reverberated through the hall.

'Turning the staircase lights on.' And with a bleep, the stairs were illuminated.

'It's a digital assistant,' Robin sighed as she pulled herself up the steps. 'I don't know how I ever lived without one.'

'A digital assistant?' Blakey followed her up the stairs. He wanted to ask what a digital assistant was, but he didn't want to seem silly.

'You should get one,' Robin said.

'I don't like the idea of owning something I can't fix, or see,' Blakey said. 'Plus, I'm more than happy with the light switches I have.'

Up the stairs, a series of impressionist paintings decorated the wall, depicting Charlie's two famous goals in the Lancashire FA Challenge Cup final and the celebrations that followed. They must have cost a bit, Blakey assumed.

'We've had a designer in working on the baby's room,' Robin said. 'So it'll look a bit different since you last saw it.'

And boy was it different. They'd not been in the house long so they'd clearly revamped the room at warp speed. Blakey had never seen a ceiling light in the shape of the World Cup before. And the carpet wasn't carpet, it was Astroturf. And the crib was a miniature version of Wembley Stadium, which must have been custom-made. And the walls were a panorama of a football crowd.

'You giving birth to Bobby Moore or what?'

Charlie crouched over a pile of wooden slats, metal brackets and loose instructions. 'I bloody hope so,' he said, rising to his feet and squeezing his grandad.

'You like the room then?' Robin said, propping herself against a wall.

'Aye, love. It's a far cry from the box room Charlie started out in. And all this must have cost some hefty nicker.'

'Don't worry about it, Grandad,' Charlie said.

'It's okay, Blakey,' Robin said. 'Charlie's had that new first-team contract, remember? Plus the money from the new sponsors is rolling in. Especially because he's got such a big TikTok following. He's done a good job of cultivating his brand.'

Blakey pursed his lips. His brand? What does that mean? He let it go. He tried not to lecture Charlie on how to live his life.

'I'll leave you boys to it,' Robin said as she left the room. 'I've got to go vomit. Lovely to see you, Blakey.'

'Take care, love.' Blakey looked over Charlie's construction project. 'What you building, lad? Is that another cot?'

'It's supposed to be a set of drawers for the baby's clothes an' that. I need it to put all those in.' He pointed to a row of shopping bags that stretched along the wall.

Blakey peered inside the bags. 'Are these all clothes? Bloody hell, Charlie. Look at all this stuff. The kid isn't even born yet and he's got more shoes than Soft Mick.'

'Who's Soft Mick?'

'I don't know but he had a lot of shoes, apparently. Charlie, you do know that babies grow out of clothes? And money doesn't last forever. You can't keep spending like this.'

'Don't worry. There's plenty more where that came from.'

Blakey shook his head. A lecture about money wasn't why he was here. His eyes darted around the room and his throat tightened – he felt suddenly uncertain about the conversation he was about to have, but he cleared his throat.

'I'm beginning to wonder how a non-league footballer can afford this lifestyle.'

Charlie set down the Ikea instructions.

'Sponsors. Don't forget sponsors. I get all kinds of contracts.'

'And that's what I'm worried about. I bet you do get all kinds of contracts ... from all kinds of people. A local celebrity attracts all types, and not all of them are decent.'

'What are you saying?'

Blakey glanced at the doorway and lowered his voice.

'I happened to have an encounter with a certain Harry the you-know-what ...'

Charlie narrowed his eyes. 'Hammer? Grandad, why are you talking to a man like him?'

'Just a random meeting, but he happened to mention your name like he knew you.'

Charlie shrugged. 'So? Lots of people know me. I'm a footballer. Anything else?'

'Well, that was it really. But the way Harry mentioned you made me concerned. I thought I'd come over and ask if there's anything I need to know.'

'Know about what?'

'Everything. Anything.'

Charlie stared into the heap of Ikea bric-a-brac and sighed. 'If you must know, there is one thing. It's nothing really ... well, it's not strictly legal but no one's getting hurt. Just a few match day favours for Harry. He pays too well to turn it down.'

'You're not talking about … match fixing?'

Charlie hung his head. 'I wouldn't call it "fixing" …'

Blakey suddenly felt unable to talk. His throat constricted around his vocal cords and he felt he ought to sit down. Charlie continued.

'Honestly, it's nothing bad in the grand scheme of things, but it pays well and it means I can provide for Robin and little Rashford. I can see that look on your face but hear me out. I want to give my kid the best life possible, but you know how it is: some doors are only open to rich folk – you know, the fancy schools and that. That's where I want to send Rashford, to a fancy school. If he or she doesn't go to these expensive places they won't get into the rich people's clubhouse. Then he'll end up broke, like everyone else around here.'

'When did you become so cynical?' Blakey fired back. 'Me and your mother were hardly millionaires and you turned out alright. You can still lead a decent life without being rich, you know.'

'I want more than decent. I want good. I want great.'

Blakey felt a knot of hypocrisy form in his stomach when he heard himself say, 'Crime isn't the answer.' He felt on shaky ground when it came to moralising: earlier this year he was part of a failed bank robbery, after all.

'Look around, Grandad. Read the papers. You must see it,' Charlie said. 'If every MP, government minister and member of the royal family can have a dodgy side deal, then so can I. These days, if you've got no money, you're nothing. Take Ally, my mate from school. He's back living with his mum after losing his job at Amazon. Even though he only quit cos he was bullied but no one cares cos he's got no money to hire a lawyer.'

Blakey bit his lip.

'Times have changed, Grandad.' Charlie shrugged. 'I don't like it either. I'm lucky: I'm a footballer and I can make money for a few years till I can't play anymore. But little Rashford might not have that chance. Then what? I've got to make money while I can. Next week, I could get an injury that takes me out of the game. At best, I've probably got ten years left in me and there's no other jobs around here unless you want to get bullied at Amazon or flip burgers at McDonalds. Dodgy dealing is the only way to get ahead, so I need to make as much as possible and build a decent life now.'

Blakey's heart sank, and he felt pulled in several directions: anxious, worried, angry and more than a little scared. He didn't want to hear it, but he needed to know more. He cleared his throat. 'OK, Charlie-boy. Tell me everything.'

CHAPTER ELEVEN

'Would you like some coffee?'

It was a strange question to ask at this late hour and it stopped Geoff dead in his tracks.

'Hi there. Would you like some coffee?'

There it was again. A novel, disembodied voice. Geoff froze.

'Did you say something, love?' he yelled to the living room.

'No, darling,' Daisy hollered back.

'I thought you just asked me if I wanted some coffee?'

'How would you like your coffee?' chirped the strange, chipper voice. 'Lightly roasted, milky medium, or black tar?'

'Daisy!' Geoff yelled. 'Did you just hear someone ask about coffee?'

Daisy didn't respond. BBC News at Ten had just come on.

Geoff listened. Nothing. He stalked the kitchen looking for the source of the coffee enquiry.

'Daisy, I think I might be having a funny turn. I keep hearing questions about coffee.'

Daisy strolled in, her evening dress swaying behind her. Geoff loved the way she dressed up for a night in.

'You silly sod. It'll be my new tea and coffee machine. It's smart. It learns all about how you like your hot drinks using artificial intelligence, apparently. It'll make any hot drink. My daughter bought it for me. She says it's the future.'

'Artificial intelligence?' He took a good look at the machine nestled between the microwave and the eggs. 'A smart kettle?'

'Smart everything, my Maisie reckons. The way she carries on, if it's not connected to the internet it's useless. She'll be trying to plug me into the World Wide Web soon enough, mark my words.'

Geoff stared into the shiny metal facade. 'Hello … Are you a coffee machine?'

'I'm Joe. Your hot-drink-making assistant. How many cups of coffee would you like?'

Geoff made sure to speak as clearly as possible. 'None, thank you.'

'Nine cups coming up.'

'No. No coffee,' Geoff said in his clearest English.

'How about a hot chocolate?' said the machine.

With a roll of eyes, Daisy poured herself a glass of fizz and retreated to the couch. 'When you're done chatting up my coffee machine, you can come and keep me company.'

'It's past ten p.m.' Geoff said to the machine, his face reflected in its chrome exterior. 'I don't want any hot drinks and neither does Daisy. So you can knock off now and relax.'

'How about a green tea?'

'No one wants green tea, okay?'

'I'm sorry, I didn't get that. How many cups would you like?'

Geoff shook his head. 'No cups!'

'Nine cups coming up.'

Geoff felt his blood pressure rise. Bloody machine, he thought, taking the mick out of me. In front of my girlfriend and everything.

'No green tea,' he yelled. 'No coffee, either!' He balled his fists. 'And before you start, no fruit teas or lattes or cappuccinos. And definitely no Bovril! Nothing, understand?'

A blue light glowed under the machine and faded softly.

'Miso soup it is then.'

'No miso!' Geoff yelled. 'And keep your bloody mouth shut!'

'Calm down, Geoffrey,' Daisy called from the living room. 'It's just a coffee machine.'

'Yeah, a not-so-smart coffee machine that's going to get its block knocked off.'

Geoff showed Joe a fist and felt Daisy's hand on his arm. She pulled him away. He took a breath and realised that for a moment he was seriously considering beating up a coffee machine.

'Oh, it's got your blood boiling, hasn't it?' Daisy said. 'Come and sit with me and relax. You've had a very stressful day.'

Geoff flumped on the couch. 'It was horrible, love. They just kept staring at me. All of them. The audience, I mean. And the more they stared at me, the more I stared back at them. Hundreds of people just looking into my soul. It was horrible ... I don't know how Bob Monkhouse did it. And as for the next thing Harry wants us to do – boy, oh boy, I don't know how we're going to pull off that trick. I mean, how the hell are we supposed to smuggle someone into prison and swap him out for another prisoner?'

'I'm sure you'll find a way.' Daisy offered him a box of Thorntons. He took a truffle.

'I don't know how we're going to do it,' he said. 'It's utter madness. Harry's really getting his money's worth out of us.'

Daisy set down her Prosecco and offered him another Thorntons, holding the box out for him to make a selection. When he declined, she took him by the hand and said, 'You'll be okay, love. You always come up with a plan. Don't forget: you're a man of action. A man of danger. Oh, to think of you going toe-to-toe with the mob! You big brave man. You maverick, you. Oh, you hunk! Come here!' And she threw her arms around him and sent the Thorntons flying.

CHAPTER TWELVE

Under normal circumstances, Finley would be wide awake by six a.m. whether he wanted to be or not. No alarm clock required … unless he was completely blotto the night before, which was unfortunately the case last night. So when he lifted his head and saw it was ten a.m. and realised he was still in his armchair, dressed in yesterday's clothes, he figured the day ahead would be a long one.

A snore came from his two-seater. It appeared to be coming from a ball of red tartan.

'Johnny,' Finley croaked, 'why did you make me drink so much?'

The needle of the record player bumped against the inner groove, soundtracking Finley's feelings of bile and regret. Empty beer cans and a whisky bottle littered the floor. He set about gathering them up.

The door buzzed.

'Whoever it is can leave me alone,' he muttered as he rubbed his throbbing head. But three more times the buzzer buzzed, each longer and sounding more impatient.

Fine.

He walked to the monitor screen by the door. The feed showed the unexpected visage of Rachael Ribbons.

What the hell did she want?

'I know you're in, I saw you from the window,' Rachael said over the intercom.

Finley couldn't think. He glanced at Johnny, who was still in the foetal position, seemingly uncontactable by man or beast.

'Bollocks,' Finley cried. He stumbled towards the two-seater and laid hands on Johnny, shaking and cajoling his houseguest.

'Come on, wee man. The local press is at the door and she can't see you here or the jig is up!'

Johnny swiped him away and snuggled up to a cushion. 'Five more minutes, Dad.'

Finley went back to the monitor.

Arms crossed, Rachael stared into the camera.

'I've got all day,' she said.

'What's going on?' Johnny said, opening an eye and rubbing his head.

Finley pulled him up by the arm and marched him into a storage cupboard in the hall.

'Stay in here and keep quiet. I'll come get you when the coast is clear.'

'What?'

Finley pushed Johnny's head inside and closed the door.

Amid the almost constant buzz of the doorbell, Finley pressed the unlock button and let Rachael in.

'The quicker I get her in, the quicker I can get rid of her,' he mumbled to himself as he rearranged the couch cushions.

Seconds later, Rachael walked in.

'I am sorry to be a bother,' she said, 'but I can't get hold of Geoff, and Blakey's nowhere to be seen.'

Finley sat in his armchair and tried to pretend he wasn't suffering from a Hiroshima-level hangover.

'Nice to know I'm at the bottom of your list.'

'I saved the best till last.' Rachael flicked her hair. 'I've only popped round because my editor has this crazy idea that … well, let me start at the beginning – do you know about Johnny Crackers? And what happened at his show last night?'

She scanned the room and her eyes settled on the carpet and the litter of cans.

'Nope.'

'He's alleged to have died last night, on stage, mid-show.'

Finley tried to seem nonchalant, but he started to hiccup. 'That's news to me.'

'Is that right? Well, it all happened last night and my editor seems to think there's some kind of funny business involved …' As she scanned the floor again, the smile dropped from her face.

'Whose is that shoe?'

Finley's head was too splintered to process all the words. Her questions felt like an inquisition, the Spanish kind. He looked at his feet. His two size-eight moccasins were still in their correct place.

'What shoes?' he grunted.

'That one shoe on the floor. That one small shoe. Your feet look too big for it.'

There it was, bold as brass, a small black-and-white brogue peeking back from under the coffee table.

'Oh, that'll be ... er, my grandson's.'

'Your grandson left a shoe here?' Rachael narrowed her eyes. 'You don't talk about your family much, apart from the fact you don't see them often. What's your grandson's name?'

'Name? Yeah ... obviously. It's er, Mark.'

'And how old is Mark?'

'... Seven.' He winced. He could have said that with more certainty.

'So your seven-year-old grandson wears black-and-white brogues with a two-inch lift in the heel?'

Finley shrugged. 'Kids, eh? I can't keep up with all their trends.'

'Let me be honest with you. My editor thinks you, Geoff and Blakey were in attendance at Johnny Cracker's tragic last live performance yesterday. She also thinks that you even tried to administer first aid to him. Is that true?'

'To be totally truthful, last night is a bit of a blur. A queasy, foggy blur.' Finley tried to suppress the hiccups but failed. 'My head's in bits.' He massaged his temple. 'That bloody Joh– I mean, Geoff! That bloody Geoff can't half drink. Perhaps you better come back later when I'm in better shape?'

'So you were at the gig last night?'

The unmistakable sound of snoring cut through the cupboard door. Finley watched Rachael's head turn slowly towards the hall.

'That'll be my cat,' Finley blurted.

'Cat?'

Finley breathed a sigh of relief when the door buzzer took over the sound of the stop-start snores.

'Get the door for me, will you?' Finley let his head flop back into the headrest and closed his eyes to the sunlight coming from the window.

When his eye reopened, Blakey was stood over him saying, 'Wakey-wakey, sunshine. We've a job to do.'

Groggier than ever, Finley lifted his head. 'Oh bugger. I must have nodded off. Where's Rachael?'

'She had to dash off,' Blakey said. 'But she said she'd be back to ask me some questions later. Dunno what about, like. Ey, where's Johnny?'

Panic flushed over Finley. He looked at the cupboard. The door was open. He raced towards it but there was nothing inside apart from a mop and bucket.

'Bloody hell! Where's he gone?' Finley searched the sofa and checked the cupboard again.

'What's all the racket about?'

'I've lost Johnny!' Finley said.

'No, you haven't.' And there he was, stood by the fridge freezer holding a frozen chicken against his forehead.

'My head is banging,' he said. 'You really should buy some ice packs. Oh, and you're out of painkillers. I polished the last few off.' The creases in his suit matched the furrows in his brow as he returned to the couch and rested a foot on the coffee table. 'Have either of you seen my other shoe?'

'It's right there,' Finley said, pointing under the table. But it wasn't. It had vanished. Finley rubbed his face. Instinctively, he knew where it had gone.

'That sneaky Rachael Ribbons ... what is she up to?'

CHAPTER THIRTEEN

Daisy glided into Finley's living room and Geoff shuffled behind her.

'Hi, Blakey, Finley,' Daisy said with her usual breezy air. 'And you must be Johnny. Nice to meet you.'

Johnny gave her a tired wave.

'The door was open so we let ourselves in,' Geoff mumbled.

Blakey looked Geoff over. 'You look dreadful.'

Geoff loosened his collar. 'I didn't sleep a wink last night. My restless leg syndrome was playing up. It was like I was walking up and down the Himalayas from dusk till dawn. Marching, I was, all night. It's a wonder my legs haven't completely seized up.'

Daisy took him by the arm. 'Geoffrey's got a delicate situation at the moment, on account of all the stress. It's made his legs very irritable.'

'Well, I've got news for you,' Finley croaked. 'The stress has only just begun.' He retreated back to his armchair, easing himself into the soft leather. 'The real job starts now. But something tells me none of us are at our finest today so perhaps all we can hope for is that we get away with this without too much bother.'

'I got what you asked for,' Blakey chimed in, holding up a crumpled Waitrose bag.

'Oh, get you!' Finley said. 'Someone's moving up in the world. Waitrose, is it?'

Blakey's face flushed red. 'Charlie takes me there once a week. He insists on Waitrose these days. If it were up to me we'd be in Lidl, but it's easier to park his Range Rover in the multi-storey at Shudehill.'

Finley rolled his eyes. 'With the kind of money he's got rolling in, trouble's a-brewing.'

Blakey bobbled the way he did when he wanted to say something but didn't know how. Something was on his mind.

'Spit it out, soft lad,' Finley said.

'Yeah, soft lad,' Johnny said, reclining on the couch, frozen chicken still pressed against his forehead.

'I like you more when you're on stage,' Blakey huffed.

'I get that a lot. So what's in the shopping bag, Softy?'

Blakey bit his lip. 'You better be worth all this.'

'I am.' Johnny smiled.

Blakey tossed the bag to Finley, who scanned its contents. He checked his watch and pitched the bag to Johnny.

'We've got an appointment with Mr Bigg in an hour, so take this and get ready.'

CHAPTER FOURTEEN

Charlie heard the *Match of the Day* ringtone blare from his iPhone. The screen read 'Harry'.

''Allo, son,' Harry said in his usual baritone. It was a voice that could cut through cinder blocks, Charlie always thought.

'Ey up, Mr Bigg. You keeping well?' Charlie left Robin on the couch and moved to the expansive dining room next door, sitting at the head of a polished oak table that could easily seat a dozen people. A classic case of overbuying, Blakey told him.

'I'm okay, son. But I'll be doing a bit better this afternoon if a *certain* right-winger playing for a *certain* team got a straight red card in the seventy-seventh minute of today's game. You never know. It might happen. Easy things to get these days, red cards – a silly challenge, swearing at the ref, a high elbow … easy done.'

'A red card?'

It was clearly an invitation, perhaps an order, to get a deliberate sending off. But a red card would be way out of character, as a certain player playing for a certain team had only ever received two yellow cards over the course of an entire season. Questions would be asked. And this match of all matches? It was a crunch game, too important for something like this.

'You know, these red cards cost a lot of money,' Harry continued. 'You wouldn't know that by the way referees brandish them about but in today's market they're worth fifty k. That's a lot more than most lower-league players earn in a year.'

Charlie took a sharp breath. Fifty thousand pounds would make a nice trust fund for Rashford. But this was getting out of hand. Conceding a throw-in during the first half was one thing – a little minor thing that wasn't going to affect the game in any real way. And that time he was asked to take two shots on goal within the first fifteen minutes was perfectly harmless. He was an attacking player, after all; it was his job to try and score. But a red card? That would probably cost his team the game. And he'd have to serve a two-match ban, at least.

'I'm sure there's a lot a *certain player* can do with that money, what with a child on the way and a big house to pay for,' Harry said. 'Plus, a certain player wouldn't want the press getting wind of his little on-the-side business now, would he? So text me later and let me know if you think a red card in the seventy-seventh minute is a likely occurrence. That way I can make sure the press doesn't find out about your off-the-books income.'

And with that, the line went dead.

CHAPTER FIFTEEN

'No sodding way!'

'Don't be such a mard-arse.'

'Is this the best you could do? Look at me! I look ridiculous! And this skirt? Is this leopard print?' Johnny inspected the baggy material flopping from his waist. 'The skirt covers my feet!'

Blakey didn't want to admit it out loud, but in an act of rebellion he had purposefully selected choice items from his family's wardrobe to make Johnny look as absurd as possible. As he gazed upon his creation, he burst into laughter.

'You need a disguise, remember, so we can transport you across town without anyone recognising you.' Blakey wiped his eyes and caught his breath. 'And this is the best I could do at short notice.'

'I know, but come on! And do I really need to wear this orange wig? It looks like something off a Cabbage Patch doll.'

Blakey held his mouth: his cheeks were hurting. It actually was off a Cabbage Patch doll.

Geoff's weariness was overridden with mirth, his body tensed with laughter.

'Never mind the wig,' Geoff managed to say mid-laugh. 'Is that shirt from a Boy Scout uniform?'

Blakey howled. 'It's Charlie's from when he was a kid.'

Johnny checked himself in a mirror and observed his attire: orange wig, Boy Scout shirt and a leopard-print skirt. 'You lot are having a laugh.'

'It's about bloody time someone was,' Finley said.

Johnny seethed into the mirror. 'Harry's going to hear about this.'

'Never mind this lot,' Daisy said, gesturing at the boys. 'I think you look wonderful. A real picture.' She marched towards him. 'And it's not what you wear, it's how you wear it.' She adjusted Johnny's wig, lifted the length of his skirt and tucked in his shirt.

'Now stand upright, put a hand on your hip and walk with me,' she said. 'Heel-toe. Heel-toe. That's it, work those flip-flops. See now, don't you feel marvellous?'

Johnny checked the mirror again, shrugged and walked the room as if it were a catwalk. 'I suppose I kind of do, actually. Fine chance of anyone recognising me, too.'

'Exactly,' Finley said.

'So what now?' Daisy said.

Blakey, Finley and Geoff exchanged glances, and with a nod they agreed it was time to see Harry.

CHAPTER SIXTEEN

The joviality of dressing Johnny up had worn off by the time Blakey and co. arrived at Mr Bigg's snooker hall. Unlike the last visit, Blakey didn't feel intimidated by the dereliction of the venue. This time, he felt a growing sense of resentment about Harry's dealings with Charlie. How dare the old man compromise his grandson's career, his livelihood and his reputation. It had to stop. Inside the hall, the smell of old beer and smoke made his mood worse, but he knew he needed to be careful and keep his mouth shut. This meeting was about a separate piece of business, and it needed to stay that way. Anyway, like Charlie told him last evening, he'd sort it out himself. Blakey knew that speaking his mind when he was angry was dangerous. So he bit his tongue and let Finley do the talking – although he couldn't help but clench his fists every time Harry spoke.

'So last night went without a hitch?' Harry asked.

'I suppose,' Finley said. 'The only concern is Rachael Ribbons. She's a journalist from the *Glebe Observer*. She's been sniffing around.'

Harry's eyes narrowed and cigar smoke escaped from his lips.

'Ah, the old *Glebe Upsetter* sticking its nose in again …' he said. 'Used to be a decent newspaper that, before it was bought by that London outfit.'

'Finley reckons she stole my shoe,' Johnny said, scratching underneath his wig. 'I can't figure out why.'

Harry reclined in his chair, his eyes hard and calculating. 'She's still fairly new on the job, isn't she? I mean, covering the big stories? Perhaps I'll have someone pay her a little visit, just to introduce myself. To get her on the team, as it were.' There was a sharp bite to his words. Blakey could see how his grandson might fall for the mobster act.

'You wouldn't hurt her, would you? She's okay, is Rachael,' Geoff said.

'I wouldn't lay a finger on her: I am a gentleman, after all.'

'Of course, Harry,' Johnny said.

Blakey felt a rush of blood. 'Bollocks,' he said. '*Gentleman*, my arse.' He glared at Harry. Even from a few feet away, he felt like he was suffocating under Harry's gaze. But to hell with it. He'd said it now. 'You think you can bring us here to carry out your stupid scheme while you're destroying my lad's career? You must be mad!'

The room fell silent, like an objection had been made at a wedding, or a noise had been heard inside a coffin at a funeral. Geoff and Finley looked stunned.

A smirk played on Harry's lips as he crossed his arms. 'Dear, oh dear. The old man has an issue. Well, let me inform you that I don't make choices for your grandson. But here's a little advice – you should be proud of your boy: he knows what's best for him and his family. Besides, remember what's at stake here, and what you owe me.'

Harry's gaze irradiated the room and when Blakey glanced at the hammer resting on the desk in front of him, his temper receded like a wave falling back into the ocean. He knew he couldn't win. Between causing more damage to Charlie's career and suffering Harry's wrath, Blakey felt trapped. He stormed out, flush with wired anxiety. As he left the room, he heard Harry say, 'You boys know what needs doing. And you've only got a few hours to prepare, so pull your mate in line. We can't have him blow this delicate operation. This has to go perfectly, and it has to happen today.'

CHAPTER SEVENTEEN

Rachael sat in her office, staring at the tiny shoe she'd swiped from Finley's flat. She didn't know why she had stolen it; maybe it was proof of something? It must be, because Finley's explanation didn't add up at all. *What child wears black-and-white brogues? Finley must think I'm stupid. What is he hiding? And what does he know about Johnny's death?* She rubbed her chin. This story was turning out to be very strange.

With a sigh, she turned to her computer and searched 'Johnny Crackers'. His official web page popped up, filled with shots of the comedian dressed up in his signature tartan.

She leaned closer to the screen, squinting. There, on Johnny's feet in nearly every photo, was a pair of distinctive black-and-white brogues. No way it could be a coincidence. She zoomed into one image then examined the brogue under her desk lamp. The scuff marks and stitching were an exact match.

She sat back in her chair. The shoe belonged to Johnny Crackers and she could prove it. But if Johnny was dead, how had his shoe ended up in Finley's flat? A macabre souvenir? Is that why Finley had been so evasive? The only explanations that made any sense were that either Finley had stolen the shoe from Johnny's corpse, which didn't seem like Finley, or that Johnny had been in Finley's flat after the performance, after he supposedly died. But how? And why? Why any of this? The pieces were not falling into place. *There's a chance Johnny is still alive,* she thought, *so I either need to prove he's dead or prove he's not. But why would Johnny fake his own death? And what's his relationship with Finley anyway?*

She dug further into Johnny's online presence. Ticketmaster listed his upcoming tour dates: Birmingham, at the Frog and Peach, this Friday; Manchester, the Thirsty Scholar, on Saturday. And Liverpool's Chuckle Hut the following Tuesday.

The tour dates went on, spanning several months, ending with a night at the Edinburgh Fringe. Rachael frowned. His social media clearly hadn't been updated: there was no press release announcing his passing, no news stories, and his agent, a man named Tony Sideways, hadn't made a comment either, so it looked like Johnny's management hadn't yet caught on that he was supposed to be dead.

A Google News search brought up a recent story from the *Daily Shine*: 'Comedy Legend in Tax Charges Nightmare'. Apparently, Johnny had been avoiding his taxes for several years and was reported to owe a large five-figure sum, which was money he didn't have, according to the article. And as a result, he was in court. The gossip section of *Northern Life* claimed the judge wanted to make an example out of him, so the book was about to be thrown his way, possibly resulting in a five-year prison sentence.

She saw even more worrying rumours on the Reddit page 'Celeb Dirt', which alleged Johnny had a gambling problem and was indebted to the tune of seventy-five thousand pounds to a mobster who went by the name of Harry the Hammer.

She sat back and played with a strand of her hair, an unconscious habit when thinking deeply. Mob debt, an unpayable tax bill and the possibility of five years in prison sounded like enough reasons for someone to fake their own death, especially for a noted livewire like Johnny. But if that were true and Johnny had indeed faked his own death, then Finley, Blakey and Geoff were all in on it. She had uncovered a conspiracy, it seemed, but she needed to know more. She walked around her office, nibbling her nails. There was no point calling the police without evidence: they'd already proved they had no appetite to investigate Johnny's 'death' any further. Plus it was too early for that; it would spoil the exclusive.

The funeral! If Johnny was dead, there'd be a service somewhere. She looked up the number for Tony Sideway's Talent Inc. Surely they would know.

No answer.

She made note of the address and grabbed her coat and bag. She had a story to uncover and a comedian to find. This was turning out to be no ordinary Saturday. She fired up her Nissan Micra and set off across the East Lancs, carried along by a bubble of excitement.

CHAPTER EIGHTEEN

Blakey's Ford rattled down a winding country road, kicking up dust behind it. He gripped the steering wheel, knuckles white. As the others chatted away, he tapped the car's faulty fuel gauge and wondered if he should fill up, but decided he was in no mood to delay his obligation to Harry any longer than necessary. Just get it over with, he thought.

'This is mad,' Geoff said. 'Utterly barmy.'

'Nonsense,' Finley replied. 'It's a foolproof plan if you think about it. Now, listen up …'

Blakey tuned them out and stared at the road and overgrown hedgerows. He was too old for this. What if it all goes wrong? He shook his head, feeling an urge to visit Charlie again, but he couldn't. Not least because it was match day and Charlie would be facing off against Milton Ramblers. As much as he didn't like it, he had to focus, although he couldn't believe he had to miss game day for this. He hadn't missed a game since–

'Blakey!' Finley snapped. 'Are you listening?'

'What? Of course I am.' He glanced in the rear-view. Johnny was in the back, nervously practising his act, pulling faces and smoothing his unruly wig.

'To summarise,' Finley said, 'with Archie being Johnny's identical twin, all we need to do is get inside the prison – visiting time makes that easy – then Archie and

Johnny can swap clothes and we'll walk out with Archie with no one any the wiser. Simple.'

'Simple,' Geoff echoed, weakly.

Johnny snorted. 'You make it sound like we're about to swap some football stickers in a playground. How am I going to change clothes in a prison visiting room?' Johnny slumped in his seat. It looked like the reality of going to prison was sinking in.

'That's where my distraction plan comes in,' Finley said.

Blakey tuned them out again until he heard Finley say, 'What got into you back there, at Harry's office?'

Blakey never liked explaining himself, but the conversation was perhaps overdue.

'I had a chat with Charlie last night.'

'About what?'

'Charlie's been earning a bit extra on the side, doing favours for Harry.'

'What kind of favours?' Geoff said.

'The kind that footballers do for gangsters. Manipulating stats, like how many corners are conceded, how many shots on target, you know, the kind of thing that big-money, black-market betters thrive on.'

Finley recoiled. 'Bollocks! Not your Charlie. No way. Next you'll be telling me the Cup final was rigged.' Finley seemed to realise the implications of his comment as the words left his mouth.

A lump grew in Blakey's throat. 'Harry had the Garstang FC goalie in his pocket. He paid him to let two goals in.' Blakey's voice dropped to a whisper. 'We probably should have wondered how Charlie managed to score two goals from his only two shots in the game.'

'No way, pal!' Finley seethed. 'Money or no money, there's no way that goalie – or any goalie – was gonna get near those strikes from Charlie.'

'Maybe, but now he's got Charlie doing all kinds of things during matches and it's not right. It's not how I raised him, and if people find out what he's doing, it'll destroy his career and Harry knows it.'

Finley nodded. 'Let me see if I can have a word with Harry,' he said. 'He might listen since we're bringing up our end of this bargain. So I'm sure he'll do what's right by Charlie. I'll have a word.'

Blakey's anxiety rose and his anger returned. 'If he interferes with Charlie's career and makes him do one more stupid thing, one more dirty deal, then I'm telling you … I won't be responsible for my actions.'

'What do you mean?' Geoff said.

Blakey could only shake his head. He was too angry to talk and the prison gates loomed ahead, stark and foreboding against the clouds. There was no turning back. They were in it up to their necks.

Finley rested a hand on Blakey's shoulder and whispered, 'Don't do anything silly, mate. Leave it with me.' And he turned to the others and said, 'Let's get this over with.'

CHAPTER NINETEEN

Blakey pulled up to the gates and rolled down his window as a burly guard ambled over, clipboard in hand.

'Name and purpose of visit?' the guard asked.

Finley leaned across Blakey. 'We're here for visiting hours,' he said smoothly. 'The lady in the back is here to see her husband, Archie Butt.'

The guard scanned Johnny in the back as the diminutive comedian retreated under his Cabbage Patch wig. With a grimace, the guard made a note on his paperwork and huffed at them to proceed through the barrier.

'Archie Butt?' Geoff muttered. 'I thought Archie was your identical twin? Why's he got a different last name?'

'Mine's a stage name,' Johnny said. 'I didn't think Johnny Butt would get many laughs.'

Geoff and Finley chuckled.

'Well, not the good kind of laugh anyway,' Johnny said. 'I want people to laugh *with* me, not *at* me. Not that my brother ever laughed at anything. He's about as much fun as a tooth extraction. You just wait until you meet him. All three of you are about to meet the most boring man in the world.'

'Boring is fine by me,' Finley said. 'That's what we need to pull this off. We need this whole thing to be as low-key as possible: no wildcards, no surprises. We must not, I repeat, we must not draw any undue attention.'

'Argh!' cried Geoff.

'What the 'eck was that?' Finley said.

Geoff's face creased with discomfort.

'Is that noise you, Geoff?'

'Oh, my giddy aunt! I've got cramp in me legs!' Geoff moaned as he massaged his thighs. 'I just need to keep them moving ... Being sat in this car's playing merry hell with them. It's all that walking I do in my sleep ... oh, bugger me ...'

Finley rolled his eyes. 'Get it out of your system cos we're pulling into the visitors' car park. Game face on.'

They parked up and signed in. Fortunately, despite a slight limp, Geoff's legs seemed to have recovered by the time a prison officer led them down a corridor and into the visiting room.

It was a dismal space, with scratched metal tables and hard-looking chairs arranged in uniform rows. They were shown to an empty table where they tried to blend in with the other visitors, most of whom were too busy staring at their phones to notice them enter.

Geoff pulled a face when he saw the state of the metal seats. 'Oh, I'm sick of sitting down.'

As Finley told him what a soft lad he was being, Blakey realised he should have paid more attention to the plan. He had no idea what was supposed to happen next.

'Er, Finley, remind me of how we're supposed to do what needs doing.'

'Shush!' Finley checked over his shoulder to the two guards at the door. He leaned to the middle of the table and whispered.

'I knew you weren't paying attention. It's a good job I was listening when Harry laid it all out. Okay, so here it is. We hold tight till Archie arrives. Then …'

'Then what?' Blakey asked.

'Then we come up with a distraction.'

'A distraction?' Geoff said. 'I thought you said we needed to be low-key and draw no undue attention.'

'Exactly, apart from the bit where we create a distraction. We have to buy Archie and Johnny some time to change clothes somehow.'

'What do you have in mind?' Blakey said. 'It must be something brilliant to distract everyone in here cos we can't rely on them all staring at their mobiles the whole time. It's such a small room with so many people in it.'

'Ah,' Finley said. He pointed a finger in the air. 'That's where there's a little snag with the plan.' His face fell.

'A snag?' Geoff said.

'A snag.'

'What kind of snag?' Blakey said.

'Well, all the time I was busy remembering the plan and making sure we got here okay … I forgot to think up a distraction.'

A knot formed in Blakey's stomach.

Geoff lowered his forehead to the table.

'Oh dear,' Johnny said, beaming with a full smile. 'No distraction, eh? Looks like we needn't have bothered coming. The plan is pointless without a distraction. Isn't that a shame? But, to be honest, I was having second thoughts about taking residence in this place, so it's for the best. Still, we better stick around to say hi to old boring-bollocks while I'm here. Oh, here he comes now.'

A line of prisoners shuffled into the room, all wearing similar grey T-shirts, jumpers and jogging bottoms. The inmates made beelines for various tables and mums hugged sons, girlfriends kissed skinhead boyfriends, and a small bespectacled man with an uncanny resemblance to Johnny rolled his eyes and walked towards them.

'You must be Archie,' Finley said, extending a hand.

'Why the hell are you dressed like that, Johnny?' Archie said, ignoring the others.

Johnny opened his mouth to answer.

'Stop!' Archie said. 'I've decided it's no longer interesting. Just get me out of here.'

'We'd like to,' Geoff said, 'but there's been a bit of an oversight.'

'What?' Archie snapped.

Johnny had a twinkle in his eye. 'I'm afraid we've come a bit underprepared, on account of not being used to springing lowlifes from prison. So, long story short, you'll be staying in here and the whole adventure is over before it got started.'

'I don't care for adventures,' Archie said. 'They're unpredictable and often end in discomfort or danger.'

Finley clicked his fingers. 'Got it. I'll fake a heart attack. It's a classic distraction. I'll flop about on the floor for a bit and it'll be all eyes on me.'

'I wouldn't do that,' Archie said. 'A visitor had a heart attack in here a few months ago. The guards dragged him out of the room and put him in the prison infirmary. Only problem was, they forgot about him and the next guards that came on shift assumed he was a prisoner and threw him in a cell.'

'What happened to him?' Geoff said.

Archie pointed to the end table. 'Ask him yourself. He's over there in the prison clothes chatting to his wife. She visits once a week.'

'Hold on. How do you know what goes on in the visitors' room? Who's been visiting you?' Johnny said.

'Mum.'

'Mum!?'

'Yeah, she comes to see me once a month.'

'What!' The words wouldn't come out of Johnny's mouth quick enough. He was so stunned he looked like he was choking, so much that Blakey considered giving him the Heimlich. Eventually, Johnny found the proper speed for his words.

'She won't even come to see my shows these days. She says old age makes it too difficult for her to get out.'

Archie folded his arms. 'I suppose I've always been her favourite.'

Johnny's jaw clenched. 'You shut up. Just shut up! I know what it is: she probably thinks I'll make her laugh too much and she might injure herself. That's why she doesn't come and see me.'

'Either that or your act is about as funny as when Dad died.'

Johnny lunged across the table and swung a fist, but Finley and Blakey dragged him back.

'I'm getting the impression you two don't get on,' Blakey said.

'What tipped you off?' Johnny said. 'Now let me at him!'

A sudden hush swept over the room and the atmosphere frosted over. The silence snapped Johnny out of his rage and Blakey and Finley stopped too as all eyes were cast towards the door to where a late-arriving prisoner stood. The other inmates looked sheepishly to their laps, avoiding eye contact, but Blakey couldn't help taking a good look at the convict who seemed to rule the room. Despite the prisoner's facial tattoo – a teardrop – he looked oddly familiar. But it couldn't be. Surely not. He looked so different, could it really be him? Sure enough, by the time the man strode across the room, it was clear who it was, and the keenest evidence was his voice. There was only one person who was capable of communicating with that exact mix of superiority and disdain. It was a combination Blakey had hoped to never hear again.

'Well, well, well, if it isn't the three musketeers?'

Finley swivelled in his seat.

'Derek. Bloody. Onions.'

CHAPTER TWENTY

The former bank manager stood over Finley with his hands on his hips and his chin in the air.

Blakey gulped. The distraction plot had just hit a large, ex-bank-manager-shaped complication.

It looked like prison suited Derek. The time he'd been serving as a result of defrauding the bank didn't seem to have dented his confidence at all. His clothes fit like they were custom-made and it even looked like he'd been working out. Blakey imagined him on the prison yard, bench-pressing massive weights, smoking cigars, and high-fiving skinheads. The teardrop tattoo on his face seemed particularly menacing. To say he was thriving behind bars would be an understatement; after only a few months inside it seemed like he owned the place.

'Afternoon, Derek. Er, nice day for it,' Geoff said in his least convincing tone.

'Nice day for what? Meeting twallops like you in my gaff?'

'Tell 'em, D-man!' said one burly prisoner in the back.

'D-Man?' Finley snorted. 'The only thing you are is a ruddy … twerp … man.'

A chorus of 'Ohhhh' rang from prisoners who had now turned their faces towards the action.

'I'll have you three do-gooders know that I have a reputation to uphold in here so I can't let language like that pass in my house. So stand up so I can thump you one.'

Finley rose from his chair and Blakey felt inclined to do the same. He'd always back up Finley in a fight without hesitation, plus he was still near boiling point over Harry. Geoff clearly had a similar idea, but his legs were not as willing as the rest of his body, and he fell flat on his backside.

'Ma bloody legs!' he howled as he crashed to the floor. 'This bloody cramp!'

'Yer what?' Derek said, somewhat disarmed by the display.

'I can't get up! Someone help me. Oh, bugger!' He rolled from side to side, clutching his thighs, his face taut with agony.

Archie leapt on the tabletop. 'Never mind all that,' he yelled, 'someone bloody punch someone!' And he lashed Johnny square in the jaw.

Someone yelled 'Fight!' as Johnny fell backwards, and all hell broke loose. Fists flew. Foul language, grunts and yelps were punctuated by Geoff's cries of 'Oh, bugger my life, someone help me get up!' Blakey ducked a flying handbag that was flung by a visitor and caught sight of Finley and Derek in a death struggle on the floor. Guards flooded the room in riot gear and started clubbing heads and dragging prisoners from the room.

As Derek was pulled away, he cackled, 'You'll not get away that easy, Finley John. This is far from over. Far from over!'

Archie and Johnny were last to be pulled apart. The guards manhandled the inmate from the room, and with his glasses cocked over his face, he kicked and screamed and cursed and was hauled down the corridor. His voice echoed into the distance as he yelled, 'You idiots! I'm Johnny! You morons! You have the wrong man!'

The prison guards paid no attention, but Blakey did. He eyed the man next to him and peered under the orange wig.

'Are you ... I mean, you swapped places?'

Archie put a finger to his lips and winked. Finley did a double take and nearly fell backwards over Geoff, who was still lying prone on the floor.

'Bloody good distraction that was,' Geoff said, wheezing and sitting upright, his face tight, still massaging his legs.

Finley gathered his breath. 'It wasn't bad,' he said. 'We couldn't have planned it better. And did you see? I walloped Derek one. Good and proper. Today's been a good day.'

'Oh, my pins!' Geoff winced.

Blakey and Finley helped him up.

'I think we better scarper while we still can,' Blakey said, looking around at the pile of visitors strewn across the room. People were on tables, some hid under chairs and others lay in a heap in the corner.

'Agreed,' Archie said, rubbing his jaw. 'Exhausting, that was. Johnny wasn't for putting on those prison clothes, I can tell you that.'

'It's been a while since I was in a barn burner like that,' Finley said, limping to the door. 'Johnny was wrong about you, Archie. You're a lot more exciting than he let on.'

'A fight was the only logical thing to do, given our situation,' Archie said.

'Shame Johnny's in prison now, though,' Finley said. 'I was getting used to him being around.'

Geoff shook his head at the carnage. 'We might be joining him in a cell at this rate. I'm not sure the authorities are going to let us leave after all this.'

Blakey knew Geoff wasn't wrong, and right on cue, a middle-aged policeman in a crisp white shirt stormed into the room. Guards followed and slammed the door behind them. The officer glared at the visitors, paying special attention to Archie and his wayward orange wig and strange leopard-print skirt.

'My name is Prison Officer Panwobble, and it's safe to say that I'm not best pleased with you lot.' He walked the line as if it were a roll call. With his finely polished shoes, his perfectly knotted tie, his immaculately trimmed moustache and unflinching expression, he looked every bit the military man. The tense aura he created took Blakey back to his days as a young scout, to when he'd put super glue on the church hall's toilet seat and the Scout Master publicly scolded him while a group of kids snickered in the background.

The officer went on.

'In my twenty years on duty here, never has there ever been so much as a bad word said in my visitors' room, let alone a *riot*! What has gone on in here today is *unforgivable*. Never in the entirety of my career have I had a group of visitors leave such a *bad taste in my mouth*.'

'Sorry. Would you like a mint?' Blakey said, patting down his pockets for the Polos he wasn't sure he actually had.

'Silence! Do you understand the mountain of paperwork you've just caused me? And you three,' he singled out Blakey, Finley and Geoff. 'Men of your age really ought to know better.'

'Better?' Finley said. 'Better? Perhaps you're right. Perhaps we should know better than to let your rotten barrel of violent offenders attack us while your guards look on.' Finley puffed his chest. 'Oh, you've not got paperwork, son. Oh, no. What you've got is a lawsuit, unless of course you want to let us walk through that door and go home right now.'

Officer Panwobble's lips twitched.

'Lawsuit? That sounds like even more paperwork to me.'

'It would be,' Geoff said, 'stacks and stacks of it.'

Officer Panwobble stretched his neck out in a quick sharp motion.

'And if I let you *leave*?'

Finley tapped his nose. 'If we leave, mum's the word about all of this. Isn't that right, everybody?'

Approval murmured through the room.

The officer flexed his jaw and fixed Finley with a steely glare.

'Off you pop then, you lot. *Move it, move it, mooove it.*' And he marched them out of the prison like drunks being bounced out of a pub.

CHAPTER TWENTY-ONE

The stadium buzzed with excitement as Glebe's home fans cheered their beloved team on against Milton Ramblers. It had been a perfect afternoon for football, with sun shining brightly through the stadium and casting a warm glow over the manicured pitch. A charge was in the air, which was already thick with the scent of meat pies. The scoreboard read 1-1, a testament to the evenly poised battle the game had been so far.

'Charlie, lad!' cried a burly fan from the sidelines, his cheeks flushed with enthusiasm. 'You show 'em what you're made of!'

Charlie gave a determined nod as a bead of sweat rolled down his forehead. He knew that the game would be one he'd never forget, but not for the reasons his fellow players or the crowd might think. The seventy-seventh minute was approaching, and Charlie was having second thoughts about taking Harry's fifty thousand.

The money would go a long way.

'Oi, Charlie!' shouted his teammate, Tommy, snapping him out of a trance. 'You up for this or what? Get moving.'

Charlie gave a thumbs up and a forced smile as he ran a few paces, but in truth he felt like he was walking off the edge of a cliff, about to disappear into the abyss. He glanced at the stadium clock: seventy-two minutes played.

The seconds seemed to be ticking faster and faster. The seconds poured away.

'Alright, lads, let's bring home the three points!' yelled his coach from the sidelines.

Charlie's heart raced and his palms grew clammy. *This is not me.* Deliberately conceding a throw-in after ten minutes, like he had done in the previous game was one thing, but a red card was quite another. He didn't mind inflating his stats to earn a few extra quid, like making sure he had four shots on distance inside forty-five minutes – that was all harmless stuff that's worth decent money to the big-time gamblers. But this ...

How would Harry react if he didn't go through with it? Harry would lose money, and money was very, very important to Harry. He'd be upset, to say the least.

Charlie's legs felt heavy as he ran across the pitch, his eyes darting between the ball and the steadily approaching seventy-seventh minute. He could feel the weight of his decision pressing down on him, like an invisible load strapped to his back.

'Oi, Charlie, get yer head in the game, mate!' hollered Tommy from somewhere behind him.

'Y-yeah,' Charlie stammered, shaking his head to clear his thoughts. 'I'm on it.'

But even as he spoke, his mind was a battlefront. The endorsement deals had slowed down, despite what he'd told Blakey, but that wasn't enough to justify a black mark on his career, not to mention risking the ire of his teammates and fans.

'Charlie, mate, you alright?' asked his teammate, Billy, jogging over. 'You look like you've just shat yourself.'

'Ah, it's nothin'.' Charlie forced a laugh. 'Just nerves, I guess.'

'Alright, well, don't let it get to you.' Billy clapped him on the shoulder. 'We need you to come up with some magic. We need these three points.'

The minutes ticked away as Charlie continued to wrestle with his conscience. Seventy-five minutes. The moment of truth was fast approaching, and he still didn't know what to do. Milton Ramblers were in possession and were fast across the grass.

'Charlie!' Tommy yelled from across the field, waving him over. 'Get stuck in!'

'Right,' Charlie muttered. He wiped his brow and jogged into place. He could feel the eyes of the crowd boring into him, the deafening roar of their cheers drowning out his thoughts.

On the stroke of the seventy-sixth minute, Milton's number eight lost control of the ball and it went out of play. The ref blew the whistle and signalled for a throw-in.

Time to make a choice.

The clock ticked seventy-seven as the throw-in was taken. Time seemed to slow as the ball travelled through the air, sailing closer and closer to his opponent. Charlie weighed up his options. He knew that this decision might change his life forever.

'Family first,' Charlie whispered to himself. He gritted his teeth and lunged at the Milton Ramblers' midfielder with a two-footed challenge that would have made Eric Cantona proud.

The whistle blew. The whole crowd gasped and a chorus of boos broke out.

'Charlie, mate, what the hell are you doing!' yelled Tommy, his eyes wide with disbelief.

The fouled player rolled around clutching his ankles, his face a picture of pain. Four Milton Ramblers players ran at Charlie, pushing him, clearly shocked by the sudden aggression. The referee darted over, waving his arms like a semaphore, signalling for calm. He reached into his pocket and lifted a red card high into the air. The display was followed by a chorus of boos and jeers from fans on all sides.

'Hey, Charlie!' called out one of his teammates, a burly defender named Dixon. 'You've just gone and ruined it for us, lad!'

'Can't believe it, Charlie, I just can't.' Tommy shook his head in disgust. 'What got into you?'

'Sorry, mate,' Charlie mumbled as he trudged away, the weight of his decision settling upon him. Harry better hold up his end of the bargain, he thought as the jeers of the crowd engulfed him.

'Campbell! What the hell was that?' Glebe Town's coach scolded, his face reddening with indignation. 'What were you thinking?'

'Sorry, gaffer,' Charlie muttered, avoiding eye contact and kicking at the pristine grass beneath him. 'I don't know what came over me.'

His boots squelched on the grass as he made the long, lonely walk towards the tunnel. The crowd's faces were twisted into snarls, a multitude of animated people tormenting him. He caught a glimpse of the club's owner in the stands, his mouth agape like he'd just witnessed a streaker running across the pitch.

'Charlie, I never thought I'd see the day,' someone shouted, their voice cracking with astonishment.

Every step towards the tunnel was heavier than the last. His head hung low, unable to meet the eyes of his teammates or the disappointed fans all around. Walking into the darkness of the tunnel, the noise was a vortex behind him. In the changing room, his regret tipped over into panic as he heard the match-day commentary through the speakers on the wall.

'Goodness me!' the commentator exclaimed. 'I don't think anyone saw that coming. Charlie Campbell, known for being one of the most level-headed players on the field, has just been given a straight red for a truly horrendous tackle. It's only by some sort of miracle that the victim of the challenge has got to his feet and seems to be okay, but it was an absolutely shocking moment. What could have possessed him to make such a reckless move at this crucial point in the game?'

'Blimey, Bill, you're right,' added the co-commentator. 'I've been watching young Charlie since he first slipped on a pair of boots, and I ain't ever seen anything like this from him before. It's like he just turned into a hooligan! One can only wonder if there's more to this story than meets the eye.'

Charlie sat on the empty changing room bench and ran a hand through his hair, sweat dripping from his brow.

'Bloody 'ell, I've gone and done it now.'

CHAPTER TWENTY-TWO

Finley turned off the car radio. The shock of what he had heard had hit him like a lightning bolt. He turned to Geoff, who was open-mouthed and pale-faced.

Finley checked to see if Blakey had heard the last few minutes of football commentary. His friend was still stood by the petrol pump, nozzle in hand, whistling as he filled the car, thankfully oblivious to what had just occurred.

'We cannot let Blakey find out about this!' Finley whispered as the smell of petrol wafted into the car.

'Why? What happened?' Archie said.

'Blakey's grandson just got sent off,' Finley said.

'And Charlie never gets sent off. Which can only mean one thing …' Geoff said.

Archie nodded. 'Harry's up to his old tricks, I see.'

'Yeah, and if Blakey finds out, he's going to be furious.'

Finley felt a stress headache coming on when he thought of what might happen. 'Exactly. You heard Blakey earlier; if he knows Harry's still messing with Charlie, I don't know what he'll do.'

'Look out, here he comes,' Geoff said.

The door swung open and the car rocked as Blakey's weight hit the driver's seat.

'Forgot my wallet,' he said, fumbling around in the glove box. 'What's appo in the match?'

'Nothing!' Geoff yelped.

'Is it still one-one?'

'Dunno.'

'Turn it on then.' Blakey reached for the dial. Finley slapped his hand away. 'No! It's broken! It just broke right now. While you were filling up.'

Blakey scratched his head. 'Really? Let me have a go.'

'No!' Archie said. 'The antenna's broken. Look.' Archie jumped out of his seat, went to the front of the car and ripped the antenna off the bonnet. He climbed back inside and handed it to Blakey. 'Broken. See.'

'Did you just break the antenna off my car?'

'No.'

'Oh. Okay. Why are you all looking at me weird?'

'We're not looking at you weird.' Finley said, trying to smile but feeling his expression fall somewhere between a grin and a grimace.

'Hmmm ... well, I better go pay for the petrol. They always have the match on in the garage, so I'll have a quick listen in there.'

'No!' Finley and Geoff yelled.

'I'll pay for it!' Finley barked. 'My treat!'

'Yer what?'

'The petrol's on me. It's the least I can do after all the driving around you do for me.'

Blakey looked astonished. 'Is it my birthday or something?'

'Yes!' Geoff yelled, seemingly unable to control the volume of his voice.

'Happy birthday to you! Happy birthday to you!' Archie sang. 'I bought you a broken antenna. Hope you love it.'

Blakey glared at Finley. Then at Geoff. Then at Archie, who gave him a little wave.

'You silly buggers.' Blakey chuckled. 'I don't know what you're up to, but you're pulling my leg somehow.'

'Ha ha ha!' Finley shouted. 'Yes. That's all. We're just pulling your leg. I'm going to go pay for the fuel now. Don't try to listen to the radio!'

Finley approached the shop and wiped his brow. Smooth, he thought. We definitely got away with that.

CHAPTER TWENTY-THREE

Rachael Ribbons pulled up to number nine New Century Avenue and stepped out of the car. She smoothed down her skirt, grabbed her bag and strode towards the building's entrance, her heels clicking on the pavement. The place had seen better days, with moss-covered walls and smashed windows serving as a backdrop to an otherwise deserted part of town.

'Blimey, this place is an armpit,' she muttered under her breath as she tightened her fingers around the strap of her bag. Approaching the door, her heart raced with anticipation as she pressed the buzzer. The button didn't seem to work. Stepping back to look at the building for signs of life, she noticed the blinds were closed and all the rooms were dark. She took a walk around the side of the building, to a dingy alley littered with cigarette butts. There she found a young man dressed in an Adidas tracksuit sitting on a stack of wooden pallets.

'Excuse me. I'm looking for Tony Sideways. He's based out of this building, apparently. Do you know him?'

The man blew a puff of smoke and eyed her warily. 'What's it to you?'

She put on her most disarming smile. 'I'm Rachael. I'm here to talk about Johnny Crackers, so I just want to chat with someone that knows him, to shed some light on a few things.'

The man seemed unimpressed. He flicked his cigarette into a nearby puddle and gestured towards a door further down the alley. 'Down there. But I'll warn you, it's a madhouse today.'

'Thanks,' Rachael chirped, her curiosity ignited. She hurried down the street, wondering what she'd find behind the dirty little red door at the bottom of the alley. The faint sound of music and chatter came from inside, along with an unmistakable clink of coins. A neon sign flickered in a small window, partially hidden behind a tattered curtain. It read 'Lucky Lou's' in garish pink letters.

She raised an eyebrow. This was more than she bargained for. In for a penny, in for a pound, she thought as she pushed the door open. A wave of warm air, sweat and the scent of cheap cologne enveloped her as she stepped inside. Everywhere she looked there were people huddled around tables and one-arm bandits, intensely focused on a variety of casino games. *This is an interesting place for an entertainment manager to use for a headquarters,* she thought as she scanned the crowded room. A burly man with a scar running down one cheek appeared at her side.

'Oi, love, what brings you to Lucky Lou's?' he asked, leering at her.

'Tony Sideways,' she replied curtly. 'I'm here to ask him some questions about Johnny Crackers.'

'Good luck with that,' the man snorted. 'He's holed up in the back, in that room there. But I doubt he'll be much help to you. He's been on a losing streak all day.'

'Tony Sideways, prepare to meet Rachael Ribbons,' she muttered as she made a beeline for the door at the back.

She drove through a haze of vape smoke and the tang of cheap beer. The seedy atmosphere seemed to drip from the walls. Men in tracksuits drank bottled beer and fidgeted with playing cards. On other tables, dice were thrown and roulette wheels spun. All eyes were on the games, so she was able to slip through the room like a shadow, observing the gamblers with a mixture of fascination and sympathy. These were not the high-rolling types, that much was clear. She watched a young man with a pained expression hand over a credit card and ask for 'just another fiver's worth, if I've got it left in the account'. The dealer swiped the card and handed over a scattering of colourful plastic chips. As Rachael sidled past, she heard the young man say, 'I just need enough to pay off my electricity bill, then I'm out.'

'Excuse me, love,' she said to a young woman clad in a rather revealing outfit, 'is Tony Sideways in there?' She pointed to a door close by.

The woman eyed Rachael closely, her lashes long and her eye make-up bold. She sneered at Rachael's sensible shoes and modest dress. 'First day on the job, love?' she drawled. 'You'll need to dress up a bit if you want any business in here. But yeah, Tony's in there but he's not exactly a ray of sunshine today.'

'Thank you ever so much,' Rachael replied, suppressing a shudder at the thought of what 'job' this lady was referring to. She approached the door and couldn't help but overhear a pair of men engaged in a heated conversation inside.

'Listen 'ere, Tony,' hissed one man with a menacing voice, 'you're a bookmaker and rules is rules. Harry put the bet on in good faith. If you've got a problem with the bet, take it up with Harry. I'm just here to collect.'

She leaned her ear to the door.

'I don't care what Harry says – I'm not paying this one out.'

'Are you mad? Do you really want to end up at the bottom of the Mersey?'

'First, he takes Johnny from me for one of his jobs – my only client – and now this? You can go back to that run-down old snooker hall and tell Harry he's taking the piss.' Tony's voice was low and dangerous. Rachael had finally come within earshot of Johnny's agent and evidently she was right; there certainly seemed to be more to Johnny's 'death' than met the eye. She listened closely as the other man in the room fired back.

'Okay, if that's what you want me to tell Harry ...'

There was a pause and footsteps came towards the door. She prepared to step away.

'Stop,' Tony said, his voice seeming to crack. The footsteps backed off. 'You want the money? Fine. Take the money, but that's it. That's the last time I take a bet from Harry on anything to do with Charlie Campbell. Harry's clearly got the lad in his pocket. I should have known better. There's no way Campbell got a red on the exact minute Harry predicted without some sort of nonsense going on. I never should have taken the bet on. Lesson learnt.'

This part of the tense exchange piqued Rachael's curiosity even more. Charlie Campbell was somehow involved with these unsavoury characters. It made no sense, but it was a juicy bit of information she couldn't ignore.

'Thanks for your cooperation,' the second voice in the room said. 'I'm sure Mr Hammer will show his gratitude.'

'You mean ... a piece of the Monaco job?'

'Mr Hammer will be in touch.'

'He better be, or so help me ...' Tony's voice sounded as dark as the grave.

Harry the Hammer? That was the mobster she saw on Reddit relating to Johnny's gambling debt ...

The footsteps came closer to the door.

She dashed away, having heard enough to get several new leads. Who is Harry the Hammer? And what are his connections to Johnny and Charlie? And what's all this about Monaco?

She had to find out.

CHAPTER TWENTY-FOUR

Archie directed Blakey to drive down a narrow avenue and had them stop next to an abandoned garage and a textile outlet.

'That's my place,' Archie said with a mischievous glint in his eye. He pointed to a crumbling shop at the end of the avenue. They got out and walked the rest of the way, since a large, overflowing bin prevented Blakey from driving further.

They followed Archie's lead and, as they neared the small storefront, Finley had to check and recheck the sign above the door to be sure he was reading right.

'Butt Drugs?!' he exclaimed. 'You have a shop called Butt Drugs. What kind of place is this?'

'A pharmacy,' Archie said.

'You named your pharmacy 'Butt Drugs'?'

'What's wrong with that?' Archie said. 'Butt is a fine name. There have been many distinguished Butts over the years.'

'Like who?' Finley said.

'Nicky Butt,' offered Blakey. 'He was a good footballer, he was.'

'You're not going to get many customers with a name like that,' Finley said.

'Customers are the last thing I want,' Archie declared. 'Figure it out, Finley: this place is a mob front. What do I want actual customers for? The only reason I have a facade is if the fuzz come for a visit. It's registered as a pharmacy, so it has to at least look like one.'

'It doesn't look like much of a pharmacy to me,' Geoff said, adjusting his cap and examining the building. 'It looks like it's been through several world wars.'

Finley looked through the windows of the dilapidated shop. It looked more like a condemned building than anything resembling a functioning business. The place seemed to sag under the weight of neglect, with windows broken and some boarded up haphazardly. The faded sign above the entrance hung precariously. The letter 'B' threatened to fall and flatten a passer-by at any moment.

'Are you sure it's safe to go in there?' Finley said.

'Absolutely,' Archie replied, nodding confidently. 'This is where the magic happens.' He pulled a key from behind an outcrop of weeds and approached the shutter. 'Let's not dilly-dally.'

With a roll of metal and a firm push of the creaky door, Archie led them into the dim, musty interior.

'Good grief,' said Blakey, shaking his head. 'It's a bit of a sorry state, isn't it? My son Max would have a field day trying to fix this place up. If you need an electrician who's decent at joinery, I'll put you in touch.'

'Jeez,' Finley mumbled, trying to appear nonchalant. He wasn't sure what he was more worried about, the crumbling walls or the idea of Blakey finding out about Charlie's red card.

Blakey pulled out his mobile. 'I better call our Charlie and see how he got on today.'

Geoff's eyes sprang open and flicked towards Finley, panic flashing on his face. Finley jumped in with the best distraction he could think of.

'Say, Blakey, remember that time we went fishing and you almost caught that massive bass? How much did it weigh again?'

'Ah, I remember that,' Blakey replied, momentarily taken aback by the sudden change of subject. 'That was quite a day. That thing must've been at least ten pounds, if memory serves.'

'Ten pounds?' Geoff scoffed, joining in awkwardly. 'I'd say it was closer to twenty! After all, you always said you had a knack for catching the big 'uns.'

'Alright, chaps,' Archie said, interrupting. 'As much as I enjoy a good fish story, I've got work to do.'

Blakey fumbled with his phone, squinting at the screen.

'Speaking of fish,' Geoff chimed in, his eyes darting between Blakey and his phone, 'have you heard about Daisy's cat? Apparently, it's been stealing fish from her neighbour's pond!'

'Really?' Blakey's bushy eyebrows rose in amusement. 'That cheeky little bugger! I always knew there was something fishy about him.'

'Ha ha, yeah!' Finley agreed aggressively. 'Now put that phone away. You're like a teenager staring at that thing all the time.'

Archie flicked on a light and a single flickering bulb cast blinking shadows across the pharmacy. A faint smell of chemicals lingered in the air and clung to Finley's nostrils.

'Blimey,' Blakey muttered, squinting at the room. 'This place really hasn't seen a customer in years.'

'Or a good dusting,' Finley added, swiping a finger across a nearby shelf and inspecting the thick layer of grime on his fingertips.

'I have been in prison for the last three years,' Archie said, indignantly. 'Forgive me if I've fallen behind with the housekeeping. Besides, it was more than just a front for a pharmacist, this place. Look.' He pointed to an ancient-looking slushy machine. 'Butt Shake, anyone? I can do cherry or bubble gum flavour.'

'Butt Shake?' Geoff said. 'What do you need shakes for if you don't have customers?'

'Bubble gum it is.' Archie glanced back at Blakey, who was still pressing buttons on his phone. With a shrug, he grasped the slushy machine's lever and gave it a firm tug. A slow, grinding noise emanated from the walls as a hidden door creaked open, revealing a narrow passage beyond. Mouths agape, the group exchanged a mix of bewildered glances.

'Blimey! A secret passage!' Blakey exclaimed, his eyes wide with awe, so much so that he pocketed his phone, to Finley's relief.

The four men crept cautiously down the dim passage, feeling the temperature drop as they ventured into the mysterious depths of Butt Drugs. They emerged into a surprisingly spacious, clean, modern chamber. A laboratory.

'Good heavens,' Geoff muttered, eyeing the various vials and beakers set out across the room. 'What in the name of Nicky Butt is all this?'

'Looks like one of them meth labs,' Finley observed, his gaze darting between the sinister-looking apparatus. The illicit nature of the operation was undeniable; the air crackled with acrid criminality. 'I've seen this kind of thing on Yankee TV shows.'

'Welcome to where dreams come true,' Archie said, beaming with pride. 'It took a while to put all this together.'

'What's it for?' Geoff said.

'Drugs, obviously,' Archie said. 'Harry the Hammer is hardly known for his charity work.'

Finley tiptoed around the clandestine lab. He picked up a small vial filled with suspicious-looking pills. 'What are these?'

'Be careful!' Archie scolded, grabbing the vial out of his hand. 'That's my own top-secret recipe. It's unique to me and worth two hundred pounds a pill in the right market.'

'Two hundred pounds a pill! What market is that?' Finley said.

'Monaco!' Archie said. 'The older gentlemen high rollers over there only want the best.'

'The best what?' Geoff asked.

'Put it this way,' Archie said, 'if one of these gets stuck in your throat, you'll die of a stiff neck.'

'You mean it's ...' Geoff said.

Archie smiled. 'Forget your cocaine and your whatever else's, Archie Butt's supercharged Viagra is where the real money's at. How do you think the millionaire OAPs keep their twenty-something-year-old girlfriends happy?'

'With money?' Finley said.

'Yeah, with that an' all, but every relationship has its physical side that cannot be ignored. Old age should not be an impediment between a man and his betrothed, should it? Want to try some?'

'Give over,' Geoff scoffed.

Blakey shook his head and Finley waved away Archie's offer.

'So that's Harry's plan?' Finley said. 'Spring you from prison and have you cook up some of this stuff to sell?'

'Harry's been getting awful pressure from the casinos in Monaco that deal this stuff,' Archie said. 'That's what I've heard, anyway.'

'Well, good luck with it all,' Blakey said. 'We've done our bit and I'm glad this is over now. Mission accomplished. Harry can consider himself paid in full.'

'Yeah. A bit like your Charlie earlier today, I suppose,' Archie said.

'What!'

'Oh, dear …' Archie stammered, exchanging nervous glances with Geoff and Finley.

Finley shot a look at Blakey and felt himself start to sweat profusely.

'What's gone on?' Blakey said, glancing between them all.

'Er … nothing. Archie didn't say anything, did you, Archie?' Finley suggested weakly. 'Anyway … er, what does a man with a two-foot penis have for breakfast?' He cringed at his attempt at another distraction.

'Nice try, lads,' Blakey scoffed, shaking his head. 'I may be old, but I'm not daft. Now tell me what's going on – has something happened that I don't know about?'

The trio exchanged glances, realising the jig was up. Finley sighed and took a deep breath. 'Alright, Blakey. Charlie got a crazy red card today.'

Blakey's voice wobbled with a mixture of shock and confusion. 'What? And … you didn't tell me?'

'We didn't want you to find out like this,' Geoff said, looking genuinely apologetic. 'We were just trying to protect you.'

'By lying to me?' Blakey snapped, his face red with indignation. He glared at them, raw-eyed. 'Thanks a lot!'

'Blakey, please understand …' Finley trailed off, unable to find the words to justify his actions.

'Enough!' Blakey barked. 'I've got to go and deal with this right now.' He paced towards the exit.

'Look, Blakey,' Finley said, his voice not more than a whisper. 'We didn't want to see you get hurt. That's why we didn't tell you …'

'Besides,' Geoff added, nervously fidgeting with his sleeve. 'It's not like we were planning to keep it from you forever. We were gonna tell you once we got all this sorted.'

'Sorted?' Blakey barked a laugh. 'Don't you worry, I'm going to sort this out good and proper!'

'Blakey,' Finley started, trying to reach out to his friend. 'Stop. We really are sorry about all of this. Just take a second.'

'Save it,' Blakey snarled, yanking his arm away from Finley's grip. 'I've had enough. I'll talk with Charlie. And I'll deal with Harry.'

'Wait!' Geoff called out, but it was no use. Blakey stormed off, leaving his friends behind in the shadowy depths of the pharmacy. They could only listen as the pharmacy's entrance slammed open and shut, punctuating what felt like the end of a once-solid friendship.

CHAPTER TWENTY-FIVE

Charlie was home late. He'd deliberately waited till Robin was out of the house visiting her parents so he wouldn't have to explain what had happened or talk about what he'd done. He couldn't face Robin yet, and the idea of talking to his dad or Blakey made him feel ill. He could already hear their disappointed mumbling about how he always got himself into trouble.

He took off his match-day shirt, balled it up and threw it in the wheelie bin. He never wanted to see that thing again. He crept inside the house, double-checking that no one was home, and took a hot shower, hoping the water would wash away his guilt. As the water poured and the steam rose, his mind raced with thoughts he wished he could banish: his dad would be okay, but how could he face Robin? And how could he explain everything to Blakey? With every second, ominous feelings swirled within, and he knew they would not easily pass.

He decided to talk to Robin and tell her everything, tell her that he was in over his head. But where would he start? And Blakey? He shook his head. That was another conversation altogether.

CHAPTER TWENTY-SIX

Finley and Geoff exchanged worried glances: both knew all too well that when Blakey got this riled up, there was no telling what he might do next.

'Sorry, fellas,' Archie said, wincing. 'I didn't mean to blurt it out like that. Sorry if I caused a problem.'

'Bugger me,' Geoff said, 'I haven't seen him that mad since someone nicked his prize-winning rhubarb. You don't think he'll do anything stupid, do you?'

'Probably,' Finley nodded.

Archie's voice cracked with urgency. 'Well, you boys better get after him then, hadn't you?'

Finley left the pharmacy just in time to see Blakey's car reversing down the alley. He tried to give chase.

'He's driving like a maniac,' Geoff said, his flat cap nearly flying off his head as they rushed down the litter-filled alley, the smell of damp mixing with a stench emanating from the large bin. Finley's feet pounded the worn cobblestones as they tried in vain to get Blakey's attention, waving and shouting. Pulling up breathlessly, Finley's eyes trained on the diminishing shape of Blakey's Ford.

Geoff stumbled to a stop, hands on his knees, and tried to catch his breath. 'Where do you think he's headed?' he said, wiping perspiration from his brow.

'He either wants to hear what's happened direct from Charlie ... or he's gone to Harry's,' Finley said, feeling his brow crease with worry. He knew that if they didn't catch up with him soon, there was no telling what could happen. 'I just hope we can reach him before he does something regrettable.'

Geoff's expression softened. 'We'd best catch up to him.'

'I feel like I've aged ten years just from that chase,' Finley muttered, wiping the back of his neck with a handkerchief.

'Tell me about it,' Geoff agreed, straightening up. 'Blakey would want to hear Charlie's side of the story first, don't you think?'

'Likely,' Finley said. 'Knowing Blakey.'

'Let's jump on a bus to Charlie's.' Geoff pointed towards a bus stop opposite the alley entrance. 'Hopefully we can calm Blakey down a bit. You know what he's like when he's miffed.'

'Aye,' Finley said. 'But we know him better than anyone so we can handle it.'

Finley's mind raced with potential scenarios as they crossed the street to the bus stop. As they waited, Finley silently prayed that their intervention would be enough to keep the situation from spiralling out of control.

'The next bus that goes near Charlie's is due in a few minutes,' Geoff said, squinting at the timetable.

'Good,' Finley replied, still scanning the street for any glimpse of Blakey's car despite it being long gone. He could practically feel Geoff's worry radiating off him, and it heightened his own sense of urgency.

As the bus rumbled along the uneven roads, the sun peeked through the clouds, casting a warm glow on the worn seats.

'I remember when we were young, one time me and Blakey went camping up in the Lakes,' Finley said. 'It must have been 1960-something. I woke up one morning to Blakey cooking bacon inside the tent. Next thing I knew, there were flames everywhere.' He chuckled. 'Daft sod.'

Geoff laughed, his flat cap bobbing up and down with the bumps in the road.

'He was so stubborn about not asking for help putting it out,' Finley continued. '"It's a bloody fire," I kept telling him. But he insisted he had it under control, even as the flames burnt his eyebrows.'

'Typical Blakey,' Geoff sighed, smiling fondly. 'He's always been a little too proud. I remember when he tried to make a go-kart out of an old shed and a few wheelbarrow wheels. This was years ago, when Max was young and I hardly knew Blakey,' Geoff added, his eyes crinkling with mirth. 'He was building this thing on the allotment and I tried to help him, but me, him and Max were more like the Three Stooges than master carpenters. The poor lad never did get his go-kart.'

'And how many times did he hit his thumb with a hammer?' Finley asked playfully, nudging Geoff with his elbow.

'His hammering wasn't that bad, to be fair; it was his measuring that didn't work. He ended up throwing his tape measure away. Said it must have been misprinted.'

Finley chuckled but the tremor of humour passed when Geoff added, 'No competition for Harry the Hammer, I suppose? I can't believe we got mixed up with him in the first place.'

For a moment, Finley expected the notorious mob boss to materialise out of thin air just by use of his name.

'Me neither,' he agreed, shaking his head. 'I certainly didn't have chasing after Blakey to save his grandson from a mob boss on my 2024 bingo card.'

'Life has a funny way of surprising us, doesn't it?' Geoff mused, staring pensively out the window. 'But we always manage to come out on top, don't we?'

'I think so,' Finley said, his gaze drifting back to the scenery outside. 'I hope so.'

'Aye,' Geoff said solemnly.

The bus rolled to a stop and Finley looked up to see they had arrived near Charlie's house. Their jovial mood evaporated. They had reached their destination.

'Right,' Finley said, squinting against the sunlight as he scanned the area for any sign of Blakey. 'Let's put an end to this mess.'

They walked a few streets and nervously approached the front door of Charlie's house, passing the perfect lawn. There was no sign of Blakey's car.

'He's not here,' Finley said.

'We'd best chat with Charlie anyway, since we're here,' Geoff said.

'You ready?' Finley asked, his hand hovering above the door knocker.

'As I'll ever be,' Geoff said, his voice a touch too high-pitched to sound confident.

Finley took a deep breath and rapped sharply on the door, his heart pounding in his chest.

'What if Harry the Hammer answers?' Geoff mumbled.

Finley gave him a look. 'Why on earth would Harry be at Charlie's house?'

'Dunno,' Geoff sighed, shifting his weight from one foot to the other. 'But maybe we should've brought some sort of weapon or something ... just in case.'

'Like what?' Finley snorted. 'A rolling pin? A feather duster? We're fine, Geoff. No danger.'

'Speak for yourself,' Geoff muttered under his breath, earning a withering look from Finley.

'Alright, enough,' Finley said, his expression serious once more as he knocked again, louder this time.

'What do we say when Charlie answers the door?' Geoff asked.

'"Hello, Charlie," would be a good start. Or possibly, "Good afternoon, sir. We're here to discuss your unfortunate entanglement with a dangerous criminal organisation, led by a man whose nickname includes the word 'hammer.' Can we come in for a biscuit?"' Finley deadpanned, which won him a reluctant chuckle from Geoff.

'Something like that,' Geoff agreed, rolling his eyes. 'But maybe leave out the biscuit part.'

'Fine,' Finley grumbled, as the sound of shuffling footsteps inside approached the door. 'But I thought it added a certain charm.'

'Focus,' Geoff whispered, just as the door creaked open to reveal Charlie. He hesitated at the threshold, looking forlorn and washed out.

'Alright,' he said finally, stepping back and allowing them entrance. 'Come in.'

CHAPTER TWENTY-SEVEN

By the time she got home, Rachael's mind was spinning with questions. She perched on her couch with her notepad and began writing about all she'd seen and heard. This was always her method of putting together an article: ignore the temptation to watch more *Luther*, leave the many TV remotes lying like large plastic slugs on the footrest, and think. It always starts with a brain dump. But all she could write were questions: how can I prove Johnny faked his own death? What is the significance of Monaco? How does Charlie factor into all this? How did Finley and co. get involved? There were too many loose ends, and the deadline was looming.

She scoured the newspaper's online archives, digging up everything she could on Harry the Hammer, aka Mr Bigg. There were several entries about Harry's snooker hall but as she dug deeper, old scans of articles complete with black-and-white photos filled her screen. It was clear that in the late 60s, Harry was not only a hero for his ferocious never-say-die attitude in the ring, but he was at one time a national celebrity and renowned ladies' man. After he retired, he returned to his hometown and set up the snooker hall.

Rachael sat on her sofa, nestling among coffee-stained notepads, the dim light from her laptop screen lighting her fingers as they danced across the keyboard, searching for information. She had a hunch that Mr Bigg was somehow the key that would unlock all the answers.

'Aha!' she exclaimed, as an old article from the archives caught her eye: 'Harry the Hammer: From Boxer to Boss'. Rachael zoomed in and began to read about Harry's rise to power.

The article painted a vivid picture of Harry as a young man in the late 1960s, a talented boxer with dreams of making it big. He had been a local hero, his chiselled jaw and piercing eyes making him a favourite among the fans. But it wasn't just Harry's good looks, powerful punches and the ever-present hammer logo on his shorts that had caught the attention of the underworld: it was his cunning nature and ruthless ambition.

Harry's first encounter with the criminal underworld had come after a close victory in the boxing ring. Sweaty, bruised and basking in the glow of triumph, he'd headed to the local pub to celebrate. There, he had met Frankie 'Fingers' McGee, a notorious mob boss who had a penchant for betting on fights and twirling a toothpick in his fingers. He had told the story of how he'd met Harry.

'He was always at the bar surrounded by people,' Frankie had recalled. 'I sidled up to him one night and said, "Nice work tonight, kid. I won a pretty penny on you." Harry raised his glass and gave me that smile. "All in a day's work," he said. I told him, "I could use someone like you in my organisation, someone with brains, brawn and a knack for getting things done." He was all like, "What's in it for me?" So I told him: money, power, respect and the knowledge that you're working for the top dog in town.'

Sensing an opportunity, Harry had agreed to meet with Frankie the following day to discuss his potential role in the 'organisation'. He'd have known it would be risky business, but apparently he couldn't resist the chance to rise above his humble beginnings and make a name for himself.

As Rachael read on, she could almost see young Harry in her mind's eye – ambitious, cunning and willing to do whatever it took to get ahead.

'Harry the Hammer,' she whispered to herself, clicking through page after page of yesterday's news. 'You've had quite a life.'

The clock ticked as Rachael continued her dive into Harry's past, each new piece of information weaving together a complex tapestry of crime and ambition. As the hours wore on, Rachael felt more and more certain that she was on the verge of uncovering something significant. Her eyes raked over the scans of yellowed newspaper pages, her intrigue growing with each new discovery. A few key figures began to emerge. One such character was Harry's boxing coach and mentor, old Roger Bush.

Roger had been known for his exquisite taste in clothing and an air of sophistication that had belied his humble beginnings. He had taken young Harry under his wing, teaching him not just the art of boxing but also introducing him to the darker side of life: mob culture.

'Harry "the Hammer" Scores Another Knockout' read one headline from 1968. The article recounted Harry's rise in the local boxing scene, quickly gaining national fame.

With every victory in the ring, Harry's power in the mob world had grown. Strategically, he used his charm and connections to consolidate his criminal empire, taking over rival gangs and establishing a vast network of illegal activities.

'Blimey, Harry, you were a busy lad back then, weren't you?' Rachael shook her head, imagining Harry juggling both his boxing career and mob dealings with equal ease.

As she continued her research, she found herself drawn into vivid imaginings of Harry's heyday. She imagined the deafening roar of the crowd as he landed a powerful left hook on an opponent, sending him crashing to the canvas. She could picture the sly grin on Harry's face as he made deals with seedy characters in smoke-filled back rooms, always one step ahead of his enemies.

'Harry, you were a force to be reckoned with. But what happened? What caused you to trade it all for a crumbling snooker hall?'

She felt a pang of sympathy for Harry – a man who had once been on top of the world, now living in relative obscurity.

'There's more to this story,' Rachael whispered to herself, determined to unravel the remaining mysteries of this enigmatic figure. 'And I'm going to be the one to tell it.'

One story from 2 April 1976 read 'Boxer Narrowly Escapes Police Raid' and detailed a close call between Harry and the authorities.

'Close shave, eh, Harry?' she muttered, imagining him outsmarting the police. But it wasn't just law enforcement that had posed a threat to Harry's empire: rival mob bosses had plagued his organisation as well.

'Oi, Harry!' a coarse voice boomed from Rachael's imagination, giving life to a rival mob boss named Tommy 'the Teeth' Thompson. 'You think you're the big man around 'ere, don't ya? Well, I got news for ya – you ain't untouchable!'

'Tommy,' Harry replied coolly, unfazed by the bluster. 'I never claimed to be untouchable. But then again, I've never had any problems dealing with nuisances like you.' His eyes locked onto Tommy's, daring him to make a move.

It was clear that Harry had faced his fair share of conflicts outside the ring during his life, but it was his ability to navigate these treacherous waters that had solidified his place in the criminal underworld.

But even the best have to retire. That sad day had come in the 1979. With Harry's fighting days behind him, he'd reinvented his public image to that of a successful businessman, albeit one still suspected of having connections to the crime world. The spectre of Harry clutching one of his trademark silver hammers had been known to put shivers down the spines of criminals and policemen alike. He had taken ownership of a string of lucrative nightclubs, at which Johnny Crackers was a near-permanent feature on stage.

Rachael chewed the end of her biro and collected her thoughts as the day rolled into late evening and the night began to draw in. Finally, her pen hit the paper and what sounded like a bomb exploded at her side as the living room window shattered into a thousand pieces, scattering a hail of fine crystals and jagged claws across her and over the room. The noise was a thunderclap, and the trauma of it left her trembling. The percussive blast was followed by the rattle of something skidding across the floor and coming to rest against the leg of her dining room table.

The only other sound was an unseen car revving down the street in front of her house. She trembled as she pulled her hands from around her head and looked into the afternoon light through the broken eye where once stood a window. Its iris was splintered, spiderwebbing to each corner as the breeze blew in, pushing glass daggers off the windowsill.

Slowly she turned to the dining room, charting the path of whatever was thrown through the window across the room and to the table leg. Nestling against the wood was a glinting silver hammer.

Something was tied to its handle.

Her heart was racing. Adrenaline tainted her tastebuds. She approached the hammer as if it were a loaded gun. A note was attached via an elastic band. The text read, 'For a man with a hammer, every problem is a nail'.

It made her spirit fierce and ready for war, because she knew in her heart that for a woman with a pen, every problem will be exposed.

She had only played snooker once, on a failed date in college, but suddenly she felt like she wanted a game.

CHAPTER TWENTY-EIGHT

Finley was astonished by Charlie's living room; he couldn't take his eyes off the massive white marble fireplace. It was magnificent. The whole room was white: white couch, carpet, chandelier, plus two giant vases displaying lilies. It must have been hell to clean. The smell of freshly baked scones wafted from the kitchen, but his appetite was non-existent.

'The housekeeper makes cakes and whatever every day,' Charlie said, nodding to the kitchen. 'Makes the place smell nice but I can never eat them so they usually end up in the bin. Shame, really. Take some home if you like.'

It seemed like Charlie couldn't make eye contact – either that or his shoes had become fascinating.

'No thanks, mate,' Finley began. He cleared his throat. 'You've not heard from Blakey in the last hour or so, have you?'

'Nah,' Charlie said solemnly. 'Not yet anyway.'

'What the bloody hell happened today, lad?' Finley said, shaking his head and eyeing up his own shoes.

'I screwed up.' Charlie exhaled into his hands. 'I had a choice to make and I made the wrong one. I've totally buggered everything.'

'We really need to find your grandad as soon as possible,' Geoff said. 'He found out about your sending off and flipped. He's assumed Harry put you up to it.'

Charlie rubbed his eyes and nodded.

'So it's urgent we find him,' Finley said. 'We're worried he might do something silly.'

'Aye,' Geoff agreed. 'And with Harry the Hammer involved, who knows what could happen?'

Charlie glanced at the framed photo of Blakey on the mantelpiece, showing his grandad standing proudly by his Escort. He tutted, as if he was ruing the day he let Harry get to him.

'Alright, let's not panic,' Charlie said finally, pulling out his mobile phone. 'Let's give him a call.' He dialled Blakey's number and put it on loudspeaker. All ears were on the dial tone.

'Come on, Grandad, pick up,' Charlie muttered under his breath. The ringing continued. Finally, after what felt like an eternity, the call went to voicemail.

'Typical, isn't it?' Charlie sighed. 'He'll probably call back later and complain about how expensive mobile calls are.'

'Well, you know Blakey,' Geoff said, trying to lighten the mood. 'It's not just phones he's stubborn about. Remember the time he tried to fix that old lawnmower by himself? He almost took off his foot.'

'True,' Finley said, 'but this time it's more than just his foot at stake.'

Charlie's eyes filled with concern. 'If he confronts Harry, it won't just be about a rigged football game anymore, will it?'

'Correct,' said Finley. 'We'll find him, lad, don't worry.' It was a promise he wasn't sure he could deliver.

Charlie tried calling Blakey again. 'I don't know why he has a mobile in the first place. He's never been one to answer his phone,' Charlie grumbled, looking at his phone. 'Especially when he's in the garage tinkering with that old car of his or down at the allotment.'

The call rang out again.

'Ah, the allotment!' Geoff exclaimed, a glimmer of hope in his eyes. 'He could be there right now, digging up some potatoes and muttering about the state of modern football.'

'True.' Finley scratched his chin. 'But we can't rule out the chance that he's already at the snooker hall, ready to give Harry the Hammer a piece of his mind.'

Geoff shifted in his seat on the sofa, his cap casting a shadow on his furrowed brow. 'We should split up. I'll go to the allotment, since it's closer to my place. Finley, you head to the snooker club. Charlie, you stay here in case he comes over to visit.'

'Sounds like a plan,' Finley said, standing and buttoning up his coat. 'I just hope we find him before things escalate.'

'Me too,' Charlie murmured.

'Alright then, let's get moving.' Finley clapped his hands. 'The sooner we find the bugger, the better.'

'Good luck,' Charlie said, escorting Geoff and Finley to the door.

The front door creaked open and Robin stepped inside. She looked weary but happy, her cheeks flushed from the crisp air. Her gaze swept across the hall, along the solemn faces, before coming to rest on Charlie's.

'Who's died?' she said.

Charlie shook his head and swallowed hard. 'Sorry, love, we need to talk.'

Finley and Geoff made a quiet exit, gently shutting the front door behind them.

CHAPTER TWENTY-NINE

Finley stepped off the packed bus en route to Harry's, feeling like a sardine escaping its tin. It had not been the quiet ride that he'd had with Geoff less than an hour ago: the bus was packed to the gills with football fans on their way home. It was with relief that Finley escaped the motorised madhouse and the din of chitter-chatter. Now he was directly across the street from the snooker club but some fans spilled off the bus too – their chaotic movements, all criss-crossing and play fighting, made it impossible to move.

'Oi, watch it!' one of the fans shouted as Finley tried to squeeze past.

'Sorry, mate,' Finley mumbled. He wondered if he had been as irritating when he was younger, or if this new generation was simply more exasperating. With a shrug, he decided it didn't matter – he had bigger things on his mind.

'Alright,' he muttered to himself, 'let's see what's what.' As he waited for the bus to drive on, he couldn't help but think about what would happen if someone crossed Harry. What was he even going to say to Harry if Blakey wasn't there? He'd have to make out like it was an awkward social call and ask vague questions about Blakey, hoping for exact answers.

'Come on, come on,' Finley urged the bus to drive off, tapping his foot impatiently on the pavement. Finally, the bus pulled away, revealing the snooker club in all of its run-down glory.

It was much worse than he was expecting. His eyes widened as he took in the sight before him. Police tape bisected the entrance and a white tent had been set up just outside: a forensics tent, they called them on TV. Which usually meant someone was dead. Police officers and people in white jumpsuits bustled around the entrance.

Finley felt as if vertigo was about to overwhelm him. He sat at the bus stop for a second and steadied his nerves.

'Harry the bleeding Hammer,' he mumbled to himself, shaking his head in disbelief. 'What have you done?'

He knew that getting involved with Harry would be trouble, but he didn't realise things would get this far out of hand. He had a sinking feeling that this had all been avoidable if he hadn't been so blithe about the whole thing. He bit his lip, trying to suppress a horrible sense of guilt.

He needed to find out what had happened.

'Excuse me, sir, you can't be here,' a stern-faced policeman said as Finley approached. The policeman clearly did not appreciate the rubbernecking crowd.

'Sorry, officer,' Finley replied, adjusting his coat. 'I was just wondering what happened.'

'I can't discuss an ongoing investigation,' the officer said curtly. 'Please move along.'

'Right, right,' Finley nodded, feigning disinterest. But as he turned to leave, his curiosity got the better of him. 'Has someone been hurt?' he asked, trying to sound casual.

'Sir,' the officer sighed, clearly annoyed, 'I need you to step back.'

'Sorry, sorry,' Finley repeated, retreating a few steps but still keeping an eye on the activity around the entrance. Curiosity gnawed at him, until he saw something he hoped not to see. Dreadful confirmation of his worst fears emerged from the darkness of the entrance into the daylight. It made his heart drop into his stomach: a stretcher being carried by people in white suits. And on that stretcher lay a body, covered with a sheet. He was unable to tear his eyes away as it was loaded into an ambulance. Finley's stomach knotted even tighter as he leaned forward, craning his neck for a better view inside the ambulance. A cacophony of sirens and murmured voices seemed to fade into the background as if he had been plunged underwater.

Inside the ambulance, a well-suited arm flopped out from under the sheet, revealing a familiar gold sovereign ring, glinting in the sunlight, HH on its face.

Finley's heart pounded. It wasn't Blakey after all – which could mean only one thing.

CHAPTER THIRTY

Geoff's nerves frayed as he entered the allotment. He couldn't quite put his finger on it, but something felt off. His cap felt tighter around his head than normal, for one thing.

The allotments' grounds were a riot of colour and life, with rows of carrots and cabbages jostling for space in the planters. Chirping of birds formed a cheerful symphony that should have been soothing, yet Geoff's anxiety continued to gnaw at him like a rabbit on lettuce.

'Blakey?' he called out.

No response, just the rustling of leaves in the gentle breeze as if the plants were whispering to him.

'Oi! Blakey!' He raised his voice a few notches and his words echoed through the allotments, bouncing off the sheds and greenhouses. The solitude heightened his worry, so when he discovered a trowel standing in the soil, he felt it right to proceed with it ready in hand like a weapon, just in case.

'Where are you, you old bugger?' he yelled, kicking at a clump of soil as he walked deeper into the allotments, past a fragrant rose bush that reminded him of Daisy.

'Alright there, Geoff?' a familiar voice came from behind a patch of raspberry canes. Geoff's heart skipped a beat. Was it Blakey? Or had Harry the Hammer's mob found their way here, sniffing around the allotments like a pack of feral dogs?

'Who's there?' Geoff demanded, gripping the handle of his trowel. The bushes parted, revealing Charlie.

'Blimey, you gave me a fright!' Geoff said, releasing the breath he forgot he was holding. 'I thought you were waiting at home.'

'Our wait is over,' Charlie replied. 'Blakey's done a usual. He's in his garage working on his knackered fuel gauge. Mam just called and told me. I thought I better pick you and Finley up so we could see him together. Come on, Robin's waiting in the car for us.'

'Sure,' Geoff agreed, trying to sound hopeful, but the gnawing feeling in his gut persisted. 'I can't shake the feeling that something isn't right here.'

'What do you mean?'

'I don't know,' Geoff nodded, his grip on the trowel still tight as he scanned the allotment. 'Something's just … amiss,' he muttered to himself as he wiped his brow. The birdsong that usually lifted his spirits seemed sinister today, as if it were a harbinger of hidden danger. 'Let me just have a look around for a sec.'

He approached Blakey's yard and noticed that the gate was slightly ajar, creaking gently in the wind like an eerie metronome. He pushed it open, feeling a chill run down his spine despite the warm sun overhead.

'Hello?' he called out, his voice echoing through the otherwise quiet space, shattering the fragile tranquillity.

He waited, straining his ears for any sign or sound. Nothing.

'Pull yourself together, Geoff,' Charlie said. 'He's not here.'

Geoff's eyes darted around Blakey's patch, but all he saw were beds of vegetables and neatly pruned rose bushes. But his instinct prickled like an itch he couldn't scratch. It was as if Blakey's shed, usually a beacon of warmth and laughter, had become haunted by his absence.

Geoff's footsteps crunched on the gravel as he ventured further. The wind whispered through the leaves of the trees, sending a shiver down his spine as he scanned the area and moved towards the rhubarb patch, where he knew Blakey had spent hours tending to the plants with loving dedication. The lush rhubarb was ripe for harvesting, even an amateur like Geoff could see that.

'Come on now, Geoff,' he muttered to himself, attempting to banish his growing concern. 'It's nothing, stop worrying.'

Then Geoff's eyes fell upon an unusual sight beyond the rhubarb, a spot of freshly turned earth, like a scar amid the vibrant greenery. He drew nearer and felt a chill creeping up his spine, as if the very earth beneath his feet was warning him away.

'What's that?' he gasped, squinting at it. 'This can't be good.'

'What?' Charlie came after him.

A mound of soil stood next to a deep hole, a hole which, by virtue of its dimensions, bore a striking resemblance to a grave. Its soil was still damp from recently being dug. A nearby shovel lay abandoned, as if whoever had been wielding it had fled in haste. Geoff's heart thundered in his chest. He was compelled to take a step back as fear gripped him.

'*Lieber Gott!*'

Charlie looked in the hole. 'Is that a …?'

'A … grave,' Geoff replied, his throat tightening.

The silence was shattered by the blare of a car horn.

'Charlie! Oi, Charlie! Hurry up!'

By the front gate, Robin leaned out of the Range Rover and impatiently waved them back to the car. Geoff and Charlie made their way towards her, not uttering a word.

'You'll never believe what we've found,' Geoff said, approaching the vehicle. 'Someone's been digging and it looks like a …' he hesitated, unsure whether he could bear to say the word again.

'It looked like a grave,' Charlie said, his face turning pale.

'Exactly.' Geoff gestured towards the ominous mound.

'Blimey,' Robin whispered.

'First things first, let's make sure Grandad's alright,' Charlie suggested. 'We'll pick up Finley and go see my grandad. Then we'll worry about this.'

Geoff nodded as Robin fired up the engine.

They piled into the car and sped away. Geoff glanced back through the rear window, to the receding image of the allotments bathed in the fading light of the day. The gravity of the situation weighed heavily on him, and he couldn't help but feel that things might get a whole lot worse before they got any better.

'I told him he's been a silly twat and he better not do it again. What more can I say?' Robin said, after Geoff inquired about her feelings regarding Charlie's match-rigging side business.

'Besides, what's done is done and it's not as if he's killed anyone.' This comment iced the atmosphere in the car, and they rode along at pace in complete silence. Finally, they pulled up to the snooker club, hoping to find Finley, but instead saw the police and a crowded crime scene. They stared out of the window at the hubbub.

'I don't like the look of this,' Geoff said.

Charlie gazed at the hall. Robin wound down her window.

'Finley!' she shouted.

Finley turned away from the crowd, shocked and pale.

'Get in,' Robin insisted.

And so he did, with no fuss or noise, aside from the clunk of the car door.

'What's all this?' Geoff asked.

'Harry the Hammer,' Finley murmured, his voice trembling. He couldn't stop thinking about that expensive ring on the lifeless hand and the thought of Blakey being responsible. 'Harry's dead,' he said.

The faces in front of him turned ashen, clearly wanting more information but he had no more to give.

'There's no good way to tell you this,' Geoff gulped, 'but I think we found a grave at Blakey's allotment!'

'We're not all seriously thinking Blakey's gone and offed Mr Bigg, are we?' Robin said with her eyebrows held high. 'I mean, that's a stretch, innit?'

'Who knows what people are capable of when pushed to the edge?' Finley muttered.

'Finley, mate.' Charlie leaned back. 'We shouldn't jump to conclusions.'

'Blakey might be at home now, but where's he been for the last few hours?' Geoff said ominously.

Finley was glad to hear Blakey had been located, but he couldn't bring himself to comment.

'Maybe he went to visit Max? Or perhaps he took a trip to the garden centre before he got back home and started work on his car?' Robin said.

'Maybe, but he's obviously been to the allotment,' Geoff mused.

'I don't want to believe Blakey's involved with that crime scene,' Finley admitted, his voice cracking slightly. 'But I saw a body, Geoff. Harry the Hammer was killed today, and Blakey's been awfully mad at him lately.'

'Finley,' Geoff said gently, his voice suddenly a steady anchor amid the swirling tide of Finley's emotions. 'Robin's right. After all, we've known Blakey for years and he is many things – he's stubborn, he's infuriating, but he's not a killer ... is he? What do you think, Charlie?'

Charlie was deaf to the world, his chin planted on his fist, staring into the distance beyond.

CHAPTER THIRTY-ONE

Rachael approached the snooker hall crime scene with a mix of trepidation and excitement. The flashing blue lights from the police cars cast an eerie glow over the building, illuminating the peeling paint and crumbling brickwork. The forensics tent billowed in the evening breeze like a sinister marquee, beckoning her closer.

'Blimey,' she muttered under her breath, 'it's like a scene out of *Midsomer Murders* round here.'

'Oi, watch your step, love,' called a burly policeman as she crossed the police tape. 'Don't want you trampling on any evidence now, do we?'

'Of course not, officer,' Rachael said, doing her best to appear both professional and unobtrusive, but she couldn't help but feel a little thrill at being so close to the action – this was the sort of story that she lived for. Outside, officers scurried back and forth like worker ants, their hushed conversations blending into a low hum. Amid it all, Rachael spotted Detective Inspector Buckets, the man in charge of the investigation and an old schoolfriend. They'd kept in regular contact, especially since her junior days as a press reporter as she'd often bump into him at local Magistrates' court when she was sent to cover the latest local cases for a weekly roundup article. The cases were not exactly exciting, although one memorable one revolved around the ownership of a lawnmower and an accusation that it was used without consent. It got very heated, as she recalls.

'Ah, Miss Ribbons!' DI Buckets greeted her with a weary smile. 'Not your usual beat, is it? What brings you to our humble crime scene?'

'It looks like a big story just broke,' Rachael replied, trying to sound casual.

'Indeed,' he chuckled. 'I probably shouldn't be letting you in here just yet.'

'If you don't tell, neither will I.' She smiled and tried not to sound desperate. 'I've visited crime scenes before with your permission. I know the drill.'

DI Buckets looked over his shoulder. 'The room hasn't officially been signed off yet but I think we've gathered pretty much all the evidence we need. Just try not to get underfoot, alright?'

'Scout's honour, sir,' she promised, crossing her heart.

As the door to the snooker hall creaked open, Rachael braced herself for what lay inside. Eerie wasn't the word. The snooker tables were still lit, as if in sombre tribute to their owner's passing. She brushed through, following the DI to a far-off room, evidently Harry's office and the scene of the crime.

'This is where it happened,' said the DI. 'The victim's name is Harry Bigg, age seventy-eight. Well, I'll leave you to do your work.'

The atmosphere within the office was heavy, like the air in an old church before a funeral service.

'Bit grim, isn't it?' DI Buckets said softly, following her gaze around the room. 'Never thought I'd see the day when the infamous Harry the Hammer would meet his end.'

'Neither did the rest of Glebe, I reckon,' Rachael replied, trying to shake off the shiver that ran down her spine.

'Alright, Miss Ribbons, I've got to get back to work. Don't forget – eyes and ears open but run everything by me before publishing.'

'Understood, Inspector,' Rachael nodded, watching him walk away. The crime scene stretched out before her like a puzzle waiting to be solved, and she couldn't help but feel a sense of guilt at feeling exhilarated by the challenge.

'Right,' she whispered to herself, pulling out her notepad and pen. 'Let's see what's what.'

'Blimey, Harry,' Rachael muttered under her breath, examining the spot on the floor where Harry's body had been found. The police had described the cause of death in graphic detail: blunt force trauma to the head from an object with a round edge, something like a hammer, they said. It was an ugly way to go, and she couldn't shake the image from her mind.

'Never thought I'd be standing here investigating a murder,' she mused aloud, scribbling notes in her notepad.

'Bit late for regrets now, Miss Ribbons,' quipped Fletcher, the local crime scene photographer and former freelancer for the *Observer*. He'd been lurking in the corner of the room. He adjusted his glasses and smirked at her startled reaction.

'Didn't see you there, Fletcher,' Rachael replied, trying her best to maintain a professional demeanour. 'Just thinking about what could've led to this mess. Speaking of which, do they have any ideas who might've done this? You know, potential motives or suspects?'

'Hard to say,' Fletcher sighed, adjusting the dial on his digital camera. 'You'd think a man like Harry would have a long list of enemies, but who would have actually had the guts to take him out?' he said, raising an eyebrow.

'Someone around here knows more than they're letting on. And I aim to find out who it is.'

'Alright, Columbo,' Fletcher said as he took his final photograph. 'Good luck, Miss Ribbons,' he added as he strode out of the room.

Rachael continued to process the gruesome details of Harry's death, feeling a strange mix of shock and intrigue. The severity of the crime was undeniable, but there was something almost irresistible about the challenge of solving it. She set about searching for clues.

Even with permission she felt she was skirting the law by snooping around Harry's desk. It was immaculate, made of oak with all the accoutrements of old-world style: two silver pens stood to attention in an art deco base, a tabletop cigar lighter – well-worn but elegant – sat by a cigar box next to a green banker's lamp. It was a pleasant space, scented with leather and cologne, a luxurious place to work, she thought, and she felt a sense of calm behind it until her eyes caught sight of several drops of blood on the desk's leather mat. The little dark circles, each its own size, reflected the lamplight. A sense of sadness emerged. Did Harry have family? Was there anyone that should be informed? She resolved to ask if the police had reached out to anybody. He may have been a gangster, but he was human too, and his loved ones would want to know.

She blinked herself into focus and turned her attention to the desk drawers, sliding one open to reveal a leather-bound journal with the initials HH embossed in gold on the front.

'Harry the Hammer's personal diary,' Rachael mused, leafing through the journal. She knew DI Buckets would want her to hand it over to, but she could scan a few pages beforehand. She flipped to today's date and her eyes immediately latched onto a hastily penned note: 'Keep an eye on Blakey.'

Blakey? As in, Blake Campbell? she thought. Friend of Finley John? Perhaps Mr Bigg had a reason to be suspicious of him … but why? What could Blakey have done to warrant Harry's attention?

She scribbled down a note, underlining 'Blakey/Harry – dig deeper' twice for emphasis.

'Blakey,' she muttered to herself, the name rolling around in her head like a rogue snooker ball on a well-worn table. The whole Blakey connection seemed as odd as a jam sandwich at a caviar tasting, but she couldn't deny the evidence staring back at her from Harry's journal. 'Charlie is Blakey's grandson. Right,' she mused, tapping her pen against her chin. 'Let's see what else there is in here.' In the same drawer she found a smaller, similar leather-bound book: an address book. She flipped through its pages, her eyes widened by some of the famous names listed.

She scanned for Blakey, Finley and Geoff, just to see if their addresses were listed. Yep, there they were, as was her own. She snapped the book shut in a startle of anger. She took a last look at the addresses written in stylish, slanted handwriting. She loved other people's penmanship. The unique lines always revealed something unconscious in the writer. Harry's script reminded her of her dad's, and the birthday cards he used to send her even down to the use of a fountain pen. She scrolled to the J's and there he was, Johnny Crackers. Her eyes fixed on the listing above it. The listing said: Johnny's Mum, Wendy Butt.

'Johnny Crackers' mum,' Rachael whispered, pointing to the neatly scripted address next to her name. 'Now why on earth would Harry have her address?' She tapped her finger on the address. 'I don't know, but it's certainly worth looking into.'

She found herself lost in thought, trying to piece it all together. What could Blakey and Johnny have to do with Harry's untimely demise? Something to do with Johnny's 'death' and Charlie's career. She took a deep breath. There were too many thoughts in her head, and she felt no closer to understanding any of this. Her fingers tightened around her notepad, the weight of their significance settling in her mind. Focus! she told herself. Start with the first thing. Page one: did Johnny really die on stage? No. Where is he? Once I've solved that, hopefully everything else will fit into place. Right then, she thought, bolstering herself, there's only one thing for it: I need to speak to Johnny's mum.

CHAPTER THIRTY-TWO

As Charlie, Geoff and Finley approached Blakey's garage, the scent of motor oil filled the air, mingling with the faint aroma of ale, which was customary for Blakey when he was working on the car. The rhythmic sound of tinkering echoed through the cluttered space, punctuated by the occasional metallic clink of tools.

'Oi, Blakey!' Finley called out, breaking the tension, his voice infused with the warmth of friendship yet aggressively demanding attention all the same. 'We've been chasing you all over town!'

The garage was a sanctuary of sorts, cluttered with memories and the ghosts of old machines. A workbench sprawled against one wall, weighed down by spanners, screwdrivers and all manner of mechanical contraptions. The smell of petrol felt as familiar and comforting as a well-worn leather jacket. Tools clinked and rattled as a hand rummaged through a rusty toolbox, searching for the perfect instrument to mend the fuel gauge.

Emerging from the shadows, Blakey wiped his grease-stained hands on a rag. His eyes flicked between Charlie, Geoff and Finley. A nervous energy hung about them like a cloud. 'Alright, you lot. Come in then,' he said, beckoning them into the garage. 'What's all this about?'

The trio exchanged uneasy glances before Charlie mustered the courage to speak. 'Grandad,' he began, his voice barely above a whisper, 'there's something I need to tell you, and I'm not sure how you're going to take it.'

'Out with it, lad,' Blakey said, a hint of concern creeping into his usually jovial tone. He swigged his beer, the grease from his hands staining the glass pint pot.

Charlie glanced at his feet, unable to meet his grandad's gaze. 'Well, you know how I've been involved with Harry the Hammer,' he said, his shoulders slumping under the weight of his guilt. 'Well I've …' Charlie hesitated, swallowing hard. 'Well, I've messed up. I really messed up. I've gone and done something really stupid, I mean proper stupid like …'

Geoff removed his cap and scratched his head. Finley stared at Charlie. The silence was deafening, broken by the distant rattle of a passing train.

'Charlie, lad,' Blakey said softly, his voice thick with emotion. 'I know all about it, and I won't lie to you, I'm disappointed. But we'll figure it out, together.'

'But how? It's not like I can undo what I've done. I'm just glad the other player's okay. The news said he had a scan on his ankle and it's nothing major, thankfully. He might even be back for the next game. And though Glebe held on to the draw, my name is mud.' Charlie's voice trembled as he looked to his grandfather, tears brimming in his eyes.

'No,' Blakey replied, placing a comforting hand on Charlie's shoulder. 'We all make mistakes, lad. Believe me. I should know: I've made one of my own today.'

Charlie's eyes flicked to Geoff and Finley. Despite the tense atmosphere, Geoff seemed unable to resist interjecting to lighten the mood. 'Well, Blakey, at least you didn't accidentally lock yourself in a porta-potty like I did last summer. Now that was a real stinker ...'

Finley rolled his eyes. 'Wait, Blakey, what do you mean when you say you've made a mistake?'

'I've gone and stuffed it right up, I have.'

'Are you telling us you ...' Finley stammered.

'Just one belt with a hammer is all it took. You should have seen the mess.'

Geoff's mouth was agape as he looked from Charlie to Blakey, trying to make sense of the confession. It looked like Finley wanted to talk but couldn't; his mouth flapped like a goldfish.

Charlie's heart raced. 'Don't be silly, Grandad! No, you didn't!'

'This isn't ideal,' Blakey said, 'but it's important to remember that everyone makes mistakes and there are consequences. It's part of life.' He paused for a moment, looking around the garage at the various tools and engines he'd fixed throughout the years. 'You see these old machines?' he gestured. 'They've all broken down at some point, but with a bit of care and patience, they're good as new again. That's what we'll do here: we'll fix this situation and make it right.'

The tension in the small garage dissipated slightly, replaced by the familiar warmth of camaraderie among friends. But it lasted only a moment. Finley stepped forward, stepping closer to Blakey. 'We'll help you get through this, mate. We're all family here. We are the Boomer Crew, after all. Through thick and thin. But I do think we should talk to the police, you know … to talk about Harry ….'

Blakey balled up his rag and tossed it at his toolbox. 'Not a bad idea, that, Finley,' Blakey said. 'Not a bad idea.'

'Right, then,' Charlie said, his voice determined but shaky. 'We'll go to the police station together. It's time they knew the truth.'

'Absolutely,' Blakey agreed, placing a reassuring hand on Charlie's shoulder. 'We'll stand side by side, lad.'

'A united front,' Geoff added. 'Like the A-Team, just older.'

'More like the Grey-Team,' Finley quipped, earning a chuckle from the others.

As they prepared to leave the garage, they exchanged nervous glances and reassuring smiles. Each movement was deliberate – pulling on jackets, checking pockets for wallets and keys, and offering quiet words of encouragement. As they stepped out of the garage and into the crisp afternoon air, united by friendship, loyalty and a shared sense of purpose, they were ready to face whatever consequences awaited them at the police station.

'Right, let's get a move on,' Blakey said, looking around the garage as if it might be his last chance to view his favourite place. 'No sense in dawdling.'

CHAPTER THIRTY-THREE

Rachael approached a Victorian terrace on Dunchurch Road, Knotty Ash, a calm, quiet suburban neighbourhood overlooking a vast park. As usual, she clutched her notepad with a sense of determination. Roses lined a path to Johnny's mum's door, creating an inviting runway even at this late evening hour.

'Here goes nothing,' she muttered under her breath as she rapped gently on the door.

'Coming!' called a sweet voice from within. The door opened and revealed Wendy Butt, Johnny's mother. She was a plump, kind-faced woman with a mop of curly grey hair that framed her rosy cheeks. 'Hello, dear! What can I do for you? Are you from the gas board?'

'No, Mrs Butt. I'm Rachael Ribbons, a reporter for the *Glebe Observer*. Sorry to disturb you at such an hour, but I've come to talk about your son. I was hoping to ask you a few questions. It won't take long,' Rachael explained, trying her best to appear professional.

'Oh, that daft sod,' Wendy replied, her eyes misting over slightly at the mention of her son. 'Yes, yes. Come inside.'

As Rachael stepped into the cosy living room, she couldn't help noticing the numerous pictures of Johnny adorning the walls – his infectious grin captured in various snapshots of his career. It was a bittersweet tribute to the once-beloved comedian.

'Can I offer you a cup of tea?' Wendy asked, ushering her to a floral-patterned armchair that looked like it had seen better days.

'Thank you. That would be lovely,' Rachael replied, settling into the chair as Wendy disappeared into the kitchen.

Rachael couldn't shake the feeling that Mrs Butt didn't seem like a mother in mourning. She glanced around the room, taking note of every detail. Doilies, net curtains, floral wallpaper. It reminded her of her own mum's place.

'Here we are,' Wendy announced, reappearing with a tray of tea things and a plate of mismatched biscuits. 'I hope you like Earl Grey – it's all I've got.'

'It's perfect,' Rachael said, accepting the cup with a smile. 'I'll get straight to the point if you don't mind. I'm here to learn more about your son's life and career.'

'Ah, I see,' Wendy replied, setting her own cup down. She paused for a moment, her eyes drifting to a photograph on the mantelpiece. The picture showed two young boys – identical twins – grinning mischievously as they clutched their school satchels. 'You mean Archie?' she said.

'Archie?' Rachael tried to remember if she had come across that name during her investigation. She filed the information away in her mind, realising that this was the first time she had heard that Johnny had a brother, much less a twin. Her curiosity piqued, but she decided to keep the conversation focused on Johnny for now.

'Actually, I'm here to talk about Johnny,' Rachael clarified gently. 'I'm looking into his life as a comedian and would appreciate any insights you might have about him.'

Wendy nodded, a hint of sadness touching her eyes. 'Of course, dear. Johnny was always chasing after laughter, even when he was a lad. Him and Archie were like two peas in a pod, but while Archie grew up and moved on, Johnny never quite managed to let go of the spotlight.'

As Wendy spoke, Rachael could see the memories playing out behind the old woman's eyes. She imagined a younger Wendy raising two boisterous boys who shared a love of laughter and mischief. The image brought a bittersweet smile to Rachael's face.

'Would you mind telling me more about Johnny's career? The ups, the downs, anything you can remember,' Rachael asked, leaning forward in her seat.

'Where would you like to start?' Wendy asked, her eyes still lost in memories of a time long past.

'Anywhere is fine,' Rachael replied, as she prepared herself to take note of every detail that was about to be shared.

'Let's see …' Wendy stared off into the distance, as if sorting through long-forgotten memories. 'I remember when they were both ten years old, Johnny used to impersonate the vicar during family gatherings. It was spot on, and even Archie couldn't help but laugh. Ah, but the older Johnny got the less funny he became, I'm sorry to say.'

As Rachael jotted down Wendy's recollections, she found herself smiling at the mental image of a young Johnny entertaining his family with his comedic prowess. Her reporter's instincts prompted her to dig deeper into Johnny's relationship with his brother, searching for any clues that might connect his 'death' to his estranged twin.

'Do you happen to know why Johnny and Archie drifted apart?' Rachael ventured cautiously, careful not to overstep her bounds.

'Ah, well,' Wendy hesitated, her smile fading slightly. 'That's a bit of a sore subject, dear. You see, as they grew older, their paths diverged. Johnny pursued comedy while Archie went on to become a successful businessman, until he got into a spot of bother, of course. They just … stopped seeing eye to eye, I suppose.'

'A spot of bother?'

'Jail, dear. Archie was a pharmacist, and very talented, but they prosecuted him as if he were a thug! It's all very unfortunate. It's best not to talk about such things.'

'Did Johnny and Archie ever have any disagreements or conflicts that you remember?' Rachael asked, sensing she was treading on delicate ground.

'Nothing specific comes to mind,' Wendy admitted with a sigh.

Rachael nodded thoughtfully, recording Wendy's words in her notepad.

'Ah, Johnny,' Wendy sighed wistfully, her eyes taking on a faraway look as she gazed at a framed photograph of a much younger version of her son, dressed in his comedic garb. 'He had such a talent for making people laugh when he was younger, you know? Back in the day, he could fill a room with laughter just by stepping onto the stage.'

Rachael couldn't help but feel a pang of sympathy for Johnny, who seemed to have been constantly chasing a dream that remained forever out of reach. She wondered how much of his longing for the limelight ruled his life. Perhaps he was just misunderstood, she thought.

Rachael felt her cheeks get hot and she couldn't help but stutter as she tried to ask her next question. 'Er, there is a story circulating that Johnny unfortunately passed away on stage last night, although the details are not clear.'

Wendy chuckled. 'I've not seen that part of his act since he was twelve. Not that I get out to see his shows. But even as a child when he grabbed his heart and fell down like a sack of potatoes, you couldn't help but think he was dead!'

'So you think it was part of the act?'

'I know so, dear. After all, if he's dead, how could he have called me earlier today?'

'Today?'

'Yes. He calls from time to time and today he was up to his old tricks; you know he's such a prankster. This time he was trying to tell me that he's in prison – would you believe that! He's always coming up with fanciful stories. He once called to tell me he'd been chosen to be the next James Bond. Anyway, this time he said he'd somehow swapped places with Archie.' She shook her head. 'I just don't get his sense of humour sometimes.'

This was enough to stop the words in Rachael's mouth. According to this call, Johnny was alive and Archie was no longer residing in the jail cell Her Majesty's court selected for him.

'Mrs Butt, what if that call wasn't a joke? What if Johnny had somehow taken Archie's place in jail? That would mean–'

'Oh dear! I see …' Wendy fretted with the hem of her blouse and thought deeply. 'Well, it serves him right for pulling my leg all the time.'

Although grateful to Wendy, Rachael grew desperate to make a polite excuse and leave to pursue this new angle.

CHAPTER THIRTY-FOUR

'Right, back to the office.' Rachael started her car and manoeuvred out of the narrow street. 'Time to put my nose to the grindstone.'

As she drove, her thoughts raced alongside her, each bend in the road revealing fresh possibilities and new angles on the story. She drummed her fingers on the steering wheel, her mind abuzz with questions about Johnny and Archie's relationship, their shared past and the dark undercurrents that might connect them both to the criminal underworld.

What if they were both involved with Harry the Hammer? she pondered, navigating a tight corner. It was a tantalising thought.

She pulled into the small car park behind the *Glebe Observer's* office. With a renewed sense of purpose, she grabbed her notepad and leapt from the car, barely remembering to lock the door behind her.

'Right, then,' she whispered to herself, striding purposefully through the empty newsroom, all the other staff had signed off for the evening. Rachael settled into her well-worn chair and began to comb through her notes. She had to get the main logic of the story on paper before she decided on the next step. She typed with fervour, the soft glow of her computer screen lighting her face.

'Ah, Archie,' she muttered under her breath, her eyes scanning through the digital archives. 'What secrets are you hiding, you cheeky little chappie?'

She clicked on a small story, filed under 'Archie Butt, criminal'. And then, just as the newsroom's energy began to wane, it appeared in front of her. A small, seemingly insignificant detail buried within an old police report.

'Gotcha,' she whispered triumphantly. The stakes had just been raised, and Rachael knew she was onto something big. She could feel it.

'Somebody's got some explaining to do,' she thought as she grabbed her bag and headed back out on the beat, this time to blow the story wide open.

CHAPTER THIRTY-FIVE

The warm, amber glow of the pub embraced the Boomer Crew boys like a comfort blanket as they gathered around an aged, wooden table. A lively conversation bubbled up from the group, their voices mingling with the hushed hum of other patrons.

'Look, I'm not saying it's the brightest idea, but I'm just saying we ought to have a pint before we toddle off to the police station,' Finley said, leaning back in his seat, one hand gesturing emphatically. 'A bit of Dutch courage never hurt anyone.'

Geoff nodded sagely. 'Besides, it's only fair we give ourselves a brief stay of execution before it all gets serious.'

'Agreed,' Blakey chimed in. 'Can't go to the authorities with a parched throat, can we?'

'Alright, alright, you've convinced me.' Charlie raised his hands in mock surrender. 'One beer, then we're off.'

As if summoned by their consensus, Al yelled over from the bar, a friendly grin splitting his weathered face. 'Evening, gents. What can I get for you lot tonight?'

'Four pints of your finest mild, please, Al,' Finley said, returning the grin. 'We need something to steady our nerves before we march off to the cop shop to make a confession.'

'Ah, well in that case you better clear your tab now.' Al winked as he worked the pump.

The police station loomed in Finley's mind like a bad debt, casting a shadow on what otherwise would be a cosy evening among friends. For now, though, he'd focus on the camaraderie and the comforting familiarity of the pub – a brief respite before plunging into the unknown.

One drink turned into two. Which turned into three, and four, which began a tipsy, sloppy conversation about other things. Charlie swirled the froth at the bottom of his pint with a mischievous grin.

'Has anyone tried that Viagra Archie's been peddling?'

'I'd sooner drink bleach,' Geoff scoffed, taking a mouthful of beer. 'I don't need anything like that.' He puffed out his chest. 'I'm all man, me, and everything still works. Ask Daisy.'

'Ah, but have you heard the rumours about what it does?' Charlie raised an eyebrow. 'Word on the street is that it's like a rocket booster for your, erm … you-know-what.'

'Is that right?' Geoff said, leaning back in thought. 'A rocket booster? I wonder what that means.' His eyes glinted with curiosity.

Finley snorted into his pint, barely suppressing a laugh. 'Sounds dangerous, if you ask me. Besides, at my age and with Ella gone, I don't see the point.'

'Come off it, Finley,' Charlie teased, nudging him playfully. 'Surely an old charmer like you could still find some use for a little chemical assistance.'

'Charmer or not, I'm not keen on having a heart attack during the act,' Finley retorted, shaking his head. 'Imagine explaining that to the nurse,' he chuckled, draining the last of his pint. 'But enough about Archie's questionable products. We've got more important matters to attend to.'

'Right you are,' Geoff nodded, setting his empty glass on the table. 'Time to face the music.'

The group stood up and prepared themselves for the task ahead.

'Wait a minute, lads,' Geoff interjected as they left the pub. 'Before we march off to the police station, how about a quick stop at Archie's place? It's on the way, after all.'

'Oh dear, here we go.' Finley frowned, his hands deep in his pockets. 'Sex mad you are.'

Geoff bounced his eyebrows and smiled. 'Just call me Mr Rocket Booster.' He was starting to slur his words a little.

'Geoff, this is hardly the time,' Blakey grumbled as he glanced nervously in the direction of the police station, his posture a little off balance on account of the booze.

'Come on, it'll only take a minute,' Geoff persisted, his persuasive nature shining through. 'Why are we in such a rush?'

Everyone shrugged.

'Fine, but make it quick,' Finley relented.

'Excellent!' Geoff grinned and led the group down a narrow, dimly lit street that sharply contrasted with the warm atmosphere they had just left behind.

They turned into the sleazy and now familiar back alley, littered with discarded rubbish and the occasional stray cat slinking past in search of scraps. The air was thick with the stench of the old bin, making each man wrinkle his nose in disgust.

'Looks like a set from a horror film,' Charlie quipped as they approached the store front.

'Let's get on with it,' Finley urged, his apprehension growing by the second. 'We've only come to satisfy Geoff's curiosity, then we're off.'

'Agreed,' Geoff nodded, his bravado faltering ever so slightly as he pushed open the door and stepped into the dilapidated pharmacy, his friends close behind. The small shop was still cluttered with dusty shelves, half-empty jars and countless boxes of expired medicine stacked precariously on top of one another.

'Welcome to the house of horrors,' Geoff whispered sarcastically in Blakey's ear, causing him to chuckle despite the eerie atmosphere.

'Oi!' barked a voice from the back of the shop. 'Watch your step!'

Emerging from behind a stack of boxes, Archie appeared, his beady eyes scanning the group suspiciously. Looking at him now, Finley found it difficult to believe he was related to a comedian. Having lost his earlier mischievous edge, Archie had a dour expression etched onto his face and an air of disinterest that made him feel distinctly unwelcome.

'Ah, Archie,' Finley greeted him with a forced smile. 'Just popped by for a little chat before we head off.'

'Chat?' Archie raised an eyebrow. 'What's so important that it couldn't wait?'

'Er …' Finley hesitated. Geoff gave him a subtle nod, urging him to continue. 'Well, you see, we're on our way to the police station.' He lowered his voice to a whisper, glancing over his shoulder to see Blakey was lost in a conversation with Charlie. 'Blakey has something he needs to get off his chest – a confession, if you will.'

'Confession?' Archie's eyes widened. 'Is he going to the fuzz voluntarily? What's he done now?'

'Murder,' Finley replied sternly, trying to convey the gravity of the situation.

'Right,' Archie said warily, scratching his chin. 'Who's he murdered, then?'

'Harry,' mouthed Finley.

'Archie, mate,' Geoff chimed in, slurring slightly, unable to contain his curiosity any longer. 'While we're here, I've been dying to know – you don't have any of that, you know, stuff lying around, do you? I wouldn't mind, you know …'

'Absolutely,' Archie grinned. 'Something for the weekend, sir?'

'Well, I suppose. It is a Saturday night after all.'

Archie went into the hidden lab and emerged with a little pill bottle.

'I'll give you a free sample, since we're mates an' all, but steady on with these. Just take one and wait thirty minutes. Then brace yourself.'

Geoff grinned at the bottle. 'Rocket booster …'

'Well, we better be off,' Finley said, interrupting.

'Wait,' Archie said suddenly, eyes lighting up with excitement. 'You lot are going to the police station, yeah? To watch Blakey's confession?'

'Er, yes,' Finley replied hesitantly.

'Would you mind if I tagged along?' Archie asked eagerly. 'It sounds like it'll be something to watch. Might be fun. I could disguise myself so no one would recognise me. I am a fugitive, after all.'

'Disguise yourself?' Finley raised an eyebrow, scepticism clear in his voice. 'How exactly do you plan on doing that?'

'Simple,' Archie declared, rummaging through a nearby drawer and producing a fake beard and a pair of glasses. He hastily put them on and turned to face the group, grinning triumphantly. 'Ta-da! What do you think?'

'Archie, mate, you look like a cross between Santa Claus and Elton John,' Blakey said, breaking away from his chat with Charlie and suddenly paying attention.

'You'll be on his naughty list now, Grandad!' Charlie chuckled. 'So don't go breaking his heart.'

'Enough,' Finley said. 'Have we all forgotten what we are about to do? I know we've had a few pints but this is serious. We're about to walk into a police station and tell them everything. Aren't we, Blakey? It's strange that everyone is so casual after all that's gone on.'

Blakey sighed and reflected, seemingly admonishing himself for his upbeat attitude. 'You're right, pal. I guess I've been blocking it out, to be honest.'

The sun had dipped well below the horizon, casting long shadows on the alley in front of Archie's pharmacy. Finley's eyes darted around, half-expecting a nosy neighbour to pop up and interrogate them about their motley crew. But the alley remained deserted, save for the same stray cat that slinked past, eyeing them warily.

'Right then,' Geoff clapped his hands, rubbing them in anticipation. 'To the police station we go!' He glanced at Archie, who was fiddling with his beard and glasses. 'You blend in perfectly, mate. No one will suspect a thing.'

'Cheers, Geoff,' Archie replied, beaming with pride despite the sarcasm dripping from Geoff's words. The others exchanged amused glances, doing their best to smother their laughter.

'Let's get a move on,' Charlie urged.

'We don't want to keep the coppers waiting.' Blakey nodded in agreement, though his face was tinged with apprehension.

Finley couldn't help but let his mind wander. Would the police believe Blakey's confession? And if so, what would happen to him?

'Finley!' Geoff's voice snapped him out of his reverie. 'You're not going to leave us high and dry, are you?'

'Sorry, mate,' Finley replied, quickening his pace to catch up with the group. 'Just lost in thought.'

'Ah, no worries,' Geoff said, slinging an arm around Finley's shoulder. 'We're all in this together, right? The Boomer Crew.'

'Right,' Finley agreed, feeling a renewed sense of solidarity.

'You ready, Blakey?' Finley asked.

'As I'll ever be,' Blakey murmured.

The ale began to take its toll as they staggered towards the police station. Finley couldn't help but think that this was an experience he'd never forget. A hazy mix of crime confession and good times with the best group of friends he could ask for, a group of friends that would soon be broken apart. With a burp, he marched them onward.

CHAPTER THIRTY-SIX

The five of them headed down Dukes Street, their laughter and stumbles a testament to the drinks they'd had. Finley tried to steady himself on a conveniently placed lamppost but missed and took out a perfectly innocent shrub.

'Whoa there, Finley,' Geoff chuckled, grabbing his friend's arm for support. 'We don't want any casualties before we even get to the station.'

'Speak for yourself,' Blakey slurred, attempting an exaggerated salute that sent him veering into a nearby bench. The resulting clang echoed through the quiet street as he clambered back to his feet. 'I'm ready to face the fuzz with all the grace of a swan in flight.'

'More like a goose on roller skates,' muttered Geoff, shaking his head at the sight.

They staggered further; passers-by gave them a wide berth, eyeing their unsteady movements with a mixture of concern and amusement. One woman in particular hurried away from the group, whispering 'Good heavens' under her breath.

'Alright, lads,' Finley said, squinting up at the imposing facade of the police station. 'Let's try not to make too much of a scene, eh?'

'Too late for that,' Geoff mumbled, straightening his rumpled clothing.

Over the road, the police station loomed like a fortress, its dark red bricks weathered and worn from years of standing guard over the quaint town. The imposing blue door stared back as Finley and co. assembled before it, daring them to cross the threshold and enter the realm it guarded. Finley knew life wouldn't be the same after they walked inside. His thoughts raced with equal parts confusion and anticipation, trying to make sense of the predicament they found themselves in. He glanced at his companions – all of whom seemed just as out of place as he felt. It was like they'd all been dropped into a murky episode of *The Bill*.

'Right,' Blakey said, breaking the silence that had settled over them. 'I suppose we'd best get on with it. No point standing around here all day.'

Finley took a long look at his friend, a last deep look at him as a free man. 'Any final words, Blakey?'

Blakey squared his shoulders and looked to the sky. 'You never told me – what does a man with a two-foot penis have for breakfast?'

Finley grinned faintly and rested a hand on Blakey's shoulder. 'Well, this morning, I had boiled eggs.'

A laugh rippled through Blakey's body and erupted on his face. 'You're a silly bollocks, you are.'

When the black letter from Harry had appeared through his letter box, Finley never imagined it would lead to this. He could sense the nervous energy radiating off Blakey as reality took hold. They crossed the short distance from the pavement to the entrance of the police station. Blakey's hand trembled ever so slightly as it hovered over the door handle and his eyes darted back and forth as if searching for any last-minute escape. Then, with his friends at his side, he stepped through the blue door and into the unknown.

'Hey,' Finley said softly, placing a reassuring hand on Blakey's shoulder. 'We're in this together, alright?'

The moment they crossed the threshold, the mood shifted around them. Gone was the easy camaraderie of the pub; instead, the cold, sterile atmosphere of the police station settled in their bones. Anticipation crackled through the air like static electricity as they approached the front desk. Finley eyed the officer sat behind the reception desk and looked around at his friends. 'Ready to face the music?'

'Let's just hope it's not our swansong,' Blakey sighed.

The clean-pressed police officer looked the epitome of professionalism. His uniform was crisp and spotless, with every button polished to a high shine. A pair of black-rimmed glasses perched on his nose and lent him a studious air. He looked up from his paperwork, assessing the men before him with a mixture of resignation and frustration.

'Evening, gentlemen,' he said, his tone betraying a hint of exasperation. 'How can I help you?'

'Officer,' Finley began, trying to ignore the fact that the room had begun to spin ever so slightly. 'We've ... I mean friend Blakey has come to report a ... a thing.'

'Right,' the officer replied, raising an eyebrow. 'Would you care to elaborate on this *thing*?'

Geoff hiccupped and leaned forward, his cap flopping over his brow. 'Officer, before he says anything, you have to know that my mate – *hic* – excuse me, I mean, my mate … he's the best bloody bloke going.' He patted Blakey heavily on one shoulder, almost missing on the first stroke but making up for it on the second.

'Aye!' shouted Charlie, cutting off Blakey as he was about to speak. 'He's my grandad and he's the best grandad I've ever had!' Then he rested his head on the reception desk, in the crease of his elbow.

The officer rolled his eyes and said earnestly, 'Gentlemen, may I please know what your visit is in reference to.'

'Murder!' Geoff blurted, his nerves – and the alcohol – getting the better of him. 'He's only gone and murdered Harry the Hammer … wiv a hammer! Whack!' Geoff punched the palm of his hand. 'Whack!' he repeated.

Blakey staggered as if a rhino had charged at his back. 'What the chuffin' heck are you on about?'

His eyes were wide and the wisp of his remaining hair seemed to levitate.

The officer rose from his stool. 'That is a very serious allegation and I'm not sure you boys understand the gravity of what you are saying. There is an open case relating to Harry Bigg's death, so if you have any information, you need to tell me now.'

Geoff gulped, his Adam's apple bobbing like a cork in choppy waters. 'I know, that's why we're 'ere.' He leaned across the desk. 'See, I found an open grave at the allotment.'

'Allotment?' The officer's eyebrow arched as he seemingly prepared himself for what was bound to be an interesting tale.

'No you ruddy well didn't!' Blakey said, nudging Geoff, who nearly slid off the desk and on to the floor. 'That's going to be my new cabbage patch, you daft bollock.'

'You don't need a big open grave for cabbages,' Archie said, grinning. 'Guilty!' He mimed banging a gavel.

'Okay, okay, Sherlock,' Blakey said raising his hands as if confronted by a gun.

'What's the grave for, then?' Finley asked.

'It's not a grave! When I stormed off, I went to calm myself down,' Blakey said, 'so I went to the allotment and dug an angry hole. There. I admit it.' He turned to the officer. 'I've been diggin' an angry hole. A big one. A real big, angry hole.'

'An angry hole?' Geoff asked, a note of incredulity creeping into his voice.

'You do know that wasting police time is a criminal offence?' The office sighed. 'Is there any more of this nonsense?'

'Wait,' Archie said. 'Are you saying that you've been digging a hole out of anger, or that the hole itself is somehow angry?'

'Both,' Blakey burped. 'I've been diggin' it cos I'm angry, but also ... well, it's just got this feelin' about it, like it's angry too. Like it wants something ... Cabbages, probably.'

'I hate cabbages,' Charlie said, his voice muffled by his face still being planted in the flesh of his arm.

'An angry hole and angry cabbages. How does this fit with the murder of Harry the Hammer?' the officer summarised, clearly trying to piece together the puzzle they'd presented him.

'And you haven't heard the half of it!' Finley chimed in, his words carrying the weight of their bizarre night. He glanced at Blakey, who seemed to have steadied himself somewhat, and gave his friend another supportive pat on the back. 'Blakey, tell 'im about ... *the hammer.*'

'I thought we came here to talk about Charlie taking bribes for doing favours for Harry?' Blakey said, shaking his head. 'The only hammer I've got is the one I used to knock my new fuel gauge into place. The manifold bent when I was getting old one out.' He turned to the officer as if he'd appreciate the difficulty of mechanical repairs. 'So I battered it with my hammer and the thing fell apart. Totally buggered up the repair, I did.'

Finley gasped. 'Ohhh, so that's what you meant? So you didn't kill Harry?'

'I didn't even know he was dead!' Blakey said, nearly jumping out of his trousers. 'I didn't do it. Maybe you did!'

'Me?' Finley said, suddenly affronted. 'I've been busy all day looking for you.'

Archie smirked. 'A likely story. Guilty!' He banged his imaginary gavel again.

'Maybe it was Geoff!' Finley blurted.

'Oh dear.' Geoff crossed his legs and shielded his zipper. 'I knew I shouldn't have taken that Viagra.'

'Maybe it was Charlie!' Archie yelled. 'Probably was, to be fair. He must have felt trapped by Harry and thought there's only one way out ...'

All eyes turned to Charlie who, without moving an inch, promptly threw up on his shoes.

'What?' he said, falling back. 'Sorry, I threw up on your floor.'

The officer marched around the desk and walked Charlie to a seat in the waiting area opposite. Charlie slumped into the chair. Finley and Blakey gathered either side of him as the officer tried to engage Charlie.

'Charlie,' he said, 'some very serious matters have been discussed here. Is there anything you want to tell me? Something you need to get off your chest?'

Charlie's eyes stayed locked on the floor. Blakey put an arm around him, and Finley did the same.

'It were just a red card,' he said mournfully, wiping vomit from his chin.

'See!' Archie screeched. 'He didn't deny it. *Guilty!* He was so pissed off about what Harry was making him do. So whack!'

'Maybe you ought to stay the night, Charlie,' the officer said. 'We can talk about this in the morning.' He pulled Charlie up by the arm. 'I have a free cell. Once you've sobered up, we'll talk about it. I'm sure the lead inspector would be very interested to hear what you have to say.' He turned to Geoff, whose eyes were wild and his trousers short. 'What's the young man's name?'

'Charlie Campbell,' Geoff said solemnly.

'Charlie Campbell, come with me …'

CHAPTER THIRTY-SEVEN

A yell came from the door. 'Wait!'

The click of heels echoed through the reception area.

The police officer rolled his eyes. 'And who are you?'

'Rachael Ribbons, *Glebe Observer*,' she announced, flipping open her notebook. 'I've come to report some information that may be of interest to you.' Her hair was slightly dishevelled, and her eyes shone with the excitement of someone who had just stumbled upon a thrilling scoop or solved a really difficult Wordle.

'Information?' Finley raised an eyebrow, curiosity piqued. 'What kind of information you got?'

'Regarding the identity of Harry the Hammer's killer,' Rachael replied, a hint of smugness in her voice.

'Go on then, love,' Finley urged. 'We're all ears.'

'Yes, I'm sure we'd all love to hear something from someone sober for a change,' the officer sneered. He sat Charlie back on a chair and faced the strident reporter.

'Very well,' Rachael said, taking a deep breath. As she opened her mouth, everyone in the room leaned in, apart from Geoff, who was on his knees by the desk, clutching his trousers. Rachael flicked through her notepad, leafing over pages then doubling back. Her brow wrinkled. 'One sec … ah, yes. Here it is: chips, biscuits, bananas … no wait, sorry that's my shopping list. I must get to Lidl before it shuts.'

'Do you know who killed Harry the Hammer or not?' the officer beseeched.

'It wasn't me, was it?' Blakey said as he slumped further into his chair.

'Nope.'

'Was it you, love?' Geoff said, still holding his trousers and clinging on to the edge of the front desk.

'I've had a funny few days,' Rachael said, glancing at her notes and pacing a few steps. 'At first, my interest was taken by the alleged death of one Mr Johnny Crackers. Someone everyone in this room knows all too well – officer excluded.' She scanned the room.

Finley tried to keep a neutral face but wasn't sure what his neutral face was supposed to feel like, so he ended up frowning.

Rachael continued. 'Through an overheard conversation with Tony Sideways – Johnny's manager – I learnt of a connection between Johnny and Harry. And when Harry turned up dead, I discovered that his murder and Johnny's whereabouts were inextricably linked.'

The room remained silent, aside from Charlie's laboured breathing and Geoff's faint complaints about his trousers being too tight.

'Officer, you may be surprised to learn that Johnny Crackers is not dead.'

'Johnny killed Harry then?' Blakey muttered.

'No. Johnny is in prison, where he's currently occupying the cell his brother should be in.' She reached for the edge of Archie's poorly fitted beard and, with one swift motion, yanked it clean off his face.

'Officer, may I present to you an escaped prisoner and murderer, Archie Butt!'

Gasps and murmurs rippled among the boys.

'Love, I'll be honest,' the officer said, 'I didn't follow a word of that.'

She pointed at Archie. 'He killed Harry!'

'Did he? Why?'

Archie bolted for the exit, tripped over Geoff's stray leg, landed on his stomach and slid across the floor. The officer helped him up.

'Did you really do what she said you did?' the officer asked Archie.

'Of bloody course I did.'

'I've heard enough,' the officer said. 'Come with me into that cell.'

'But why did you do it?' Blakey asked.

'Why do you think? There was a reason I was in prison in the first place, you know?'

'For rotten Viagra!' Geoff yelled.

'No,' Archie said as the officer cuffed his hands behind his back. 'I was inside cos I like to kill people and he left a hammer right there on his desk. It was basically an invitation.' He shook his head. 'I knew it was a mistake coming in here, but I thought Blakey was going to say *he* killed Harry, and I didn't want to miss that show. Hey-ho, prison ain't too bad.' And he smiled a gleaming smile as he was led away into the bowels of the police station.

CHAPTER THIRTY-EIGHT

'Good morning, love. You okay?' Finley said as he cleared away the leaves and twigs from Ella's tombstone. The breeze was soft as it dipped and weaved through the graveyard, pushing the trees into a gentle dance. The morning was early, the air was refreshing and, as usual, the graveyard was at peace.

'Ah, you wouldn't believe the night I had … I hardly know where to start cos I'm all bloody hungover, of course. I know, you're right: I really need to stop overdoing it … Oh, I got these for you.'

He laid down a bundle of wildflowers near her and breathed a heavy sigh.

'Charlie's been a silly boy this week. Yeah. He got wrapped up with a man called Harry, an old boxer, second name Bigg. I know you're not much into boxing but if you see him up there say hello from me. The poor fella passed away yesterday. Like I said, it's been a mad old week. Anyway, in terms of Charlie, today's paper says it all.'

He pulled a rolled-up newspaper from his pocket, the Sunday edition of the *Glebe Observer*.

'Look at that back page, love. "Red Card Charlie" they're calling him now. Ha. Silly sod. He'll be alright. Everyone will have forgotten all about it by this afternoon.'

He rolled the paper up, put it away and looked at the deep cuts of the engraved words on his wife's headstone. He felt his chin crease, his heart swell and his eyes tear up.

'I bloody miss you, love.'

He let the tears fall. Drying his eyes, he held the handkerchief to his face and tried not to cry again.

'I met a bloke called Johnny,' he said as he blew his nose. 'In fact, you'll remember him. He was the short, funny bloke on telly years ago. A stand-up comedian wearing red tartan ... Yeah, that's the one. Well, he did a short stint in the nick this week, but I think he'll be out again soon. Although he'll still have trouble with the Inland Revenue, I think, so I'm not sure what he'll do about that.'

He wiped his nose again.

'I know, love, I know ... Look at me mixing with celebrities. And that's not the only person I've been mixing with. Don't worry, nothing like that. What I mean is, I've got a visitor for you. She's a bit upset but here she comes now.'

Finley gestured for his daughter, Lisa, to come alongside. He put an arm around her as she cried into a tissue.

'I'm sorry it's been a while, Mum.'

Finley handed her a clean hanky, and they cried together in bursts between brief moments of calm, and they hugged for the first time in ten years.

CHAPTER THIRTY-NINE

Rachael was late to her office on Monday, as usual, but she was just in time to see the postman dump what looked like a whole sack of letters on her desk. She had spent the morning tying up loose ends before she finally put ink on the page to write the article that had proven so elusive to pin down. The focus had shifted more than once. Should it be a humorous tale of a comedian faking his own death? Or a salacious story of crime and murder? Or even some kind of semi-glamorous gangster story? She still wasn't sure.

She stared at her desk. It was practically buried beneath a mountain of letters, all shapes and sizes, forming a chaotic paper mound. She shook her head in disbelief, muttering under her breath, 'Who the heck still sends letters these days? I mean, it's not my birthday or anything.'

She plonked herself down on her creaky chair and began sorting through the enormous pile. All were decorated with stamps, a charming reminder of yesteryear. She took a second to admire the handwritten addresses scrawled by a shaky hand.

'Let's see what these folks have to say,' she murmured as she picked up the first envelope. She tore it open, briefly noticing the faint scent of lavender emanating from the page as she unfolded the letter.

'Dear Miss Ribbons,' she read aloud. 'I just wanted to write to you in regard to the tragic passing of Harry Bigg...'

Her mind raced with the details of her investigation into the notorious mob boss. She read on.

'I know how people thought of Harry, and I figured the paper would be writing about him so I wanted to let you know about how he helped my elderly mother when she fell and broke her hip ...' Rachael paused, swallowing hard. 'I thought you ought to know that even though he had a fearsome reputation, he was also capable of honest kindness.'

She reached for another letter. The other offices were silent, save for the occasional clink of a coffee mug. The voices lifted off the page, one after another, all clamouring to be heard.

'... I'll never forget how Harry helped me find my dog, Franco, when he went missing ...'

'During lockdown, Harry personally delivered groceries to my mum ...'

'When my dad needed private care after he fell ill with Alzheimer's, Harry stepped in ...'

She felt captivated by the rapidly evolving portrait of Harry the Hammer, and how these people just wanted their voices heard.

Letter after letter detailed Harry's previously unknown good deeds and it made her heart swell with admiration for the complex figure at the centre of these moving tales. As she sifted through the remaining letters, she knew that she couldn't let these stories go untold. Harry the Hammer may have been a man of contradictions, but beneath the tough exterior had lain a beating heart that had touched the lives of so many in unexpected ways.

'Right then,' she thought. 'Looks like I've got the angle of my article sorted. It's time to share these stories and show the world the real Mr Harry Bigg.'

CHAPTER FORTY

'I still can't believe you thought I killed Harry,' Blakey said as he settled on Finley's two-seater.

'I'm ruddy glad you didn't,' Finley chuckled as he blew on his fresh cup of tea.

'You definitely didn't, did you?' Geoff asked sarcastically.

'No, Mr Rocket Booster. Have you recovered yet?'

'I think so. I tell you what, though, that stuff didn't half cure my restless leg syndrome. I got a solid eight hours last night.'

'Sleep, you mean?' Finley snorted.

'Aye, like a log, I was.'

A bang on the window jolted Finley and sent his brew splashing over him.

'Oh, you daft bollock!'

'Who's that?' Blakey asked.

'It might be PC World. They're due to come and repair Daisy's coffee-and-tea machine today.'

'It ain't PC World,' Finley said.

Johnny's cheeky face appeared at the window. He waved at them like a maniac.

'What's he doing here?' Geoff asked.

'I dunno, but you better let him in,' Finley said.

As Geoff unlocked the door, the sound of shoe leather clicked up the corridor and the door swung open with a cry of 'Ay up, nobheads!'

'Well, look who it isn't,' Finley said, genuinely happy to see Johnny. In a pair of jeans and a polo shirt, he looked different, but his face still shone with the same childish mischief.

'Good to see you, lad,' Blakey said.

'Aye, me an' all,' Geoff agreed.

'So you're out of jail then?' Finley said.

'They kicked me out when they found out about Archie. They're so embarrassed about him escaping they're brushing it under the table sharpish. Anyway, I thought I'd come over and see my mates.'

'I've been thinking about you and all your tax difficulties,' Finley said. 'What are you going to do about all that?'

'Ah!' Johnny smiled. 'I've got what can only be described as a perfect plan, and I've got a feeling you boys are going to be bang up for this …'

'Oh, bloody hell, what now?' Blakey moaned.

'My brother is a sociopathic killer, but he had a pretty good hustle going with those pills he made. I went round to his shop this morning for a look about and it turns out that before he got locked up again, he'd been a very busy boy. You should have a look for yourselves: there's boxes and boxes full of those pills. Hundreds of them. Thousands even. All intended for the casinos abroad.'

'So?' Geoff said.

'Well …' Johnny rubbed his hands together. 'Who fancies a trip to Monaco?'

Printed in Great Britain
by Amazon